The Landscape
Comes
and Goes

The Landscape Comes and Goes

ELIZABETH GUNN

PETER OWEN · LONDON

ISBN 0 7206 0638 1

PETER OWEN PUBLISHERS
73 Kenway Road London SW5 0RE

First published in Great Britain 1985
© Elizabeth Gunn 1985

Photoset and printed in Great Britain by
Photobooks (Bristol) Ltd

For Miranda

Oh, what a thing is man! how farre from power,
  From settled peace and rest!
He is some twenty sev'rall men at least
  Each sev'rall houre.

. . . . . .

He builds a house, which quickly down must go,
  As if a whirlwinde blew
And crusht the building; and it's partly true,
  His minde is so.

George Herbert

1

Ice lies on the land. I chose it. I'd still choose it – the frost-flowers like ferns, like fans inside my windows, and which at lunchtime will still be flowing into my towels and bathmats, penetrating meanwhile in this cold.

Yes, I'd still choose to wait (and in January it might be midnight at seven) to scrape a hole in this white winter garden, this white Douanier Rousseau forest that grows inside my house, and look out – on to what you never know. And it's possible, my friend, that you won't like what you see, that it's still so dark because there's a thick fog and not only is but has been; day after day of claustrophobia. Or possibly the beating you have taken throughout the night, the bludgeoning and buffeting will have warned you: we don't have winds here, only icy gales.

I can still remember a time when I thought the arrangement perfect, the rage of the wolf boxed inside my chimney the perfect counterpoint to Jane Austen and Trollope. The logs blazed and the shadows danced in the room with its drawn curtains, in the days when the logs blazed and the shadows danced. And I blazed the glad news abroad in the days when I still wrote letters, the days when miracles were my daily bread.

Well, I can still pot-hole in my flannel nightdress and witness the birth of a day in the life of the world, January 5th 1983, a day that tomorrow will lie with its ancestors. And it's not just the birth of a day but of the universe you see here. Soon, born of chaos and old night, high in the void you will see it emerge – black, domed, immense – a cranium of which there is neither beginning nor end. That strange mound you saw by the bridge? Yes, a terminal moraine, deposited in the ice-age and still cold, cold as iron; if you rapped on any one of these hills today I swear they'd give you back a tinkling sound. The very feet of the sheep seem frozen to the ground as they hobble to and fro on their black sticks. They are only, in fact, prodded into doing so by the knowledge that since it's now light – at eleven – hay will be coming. Earlier, when I scraped my hole, they were wedged together for warmth, still in bed, a small, square feather-bed in a field of green pearls.

Do you have green pearls in your Chobham garden? You don't? Not green. The little black dress is enjoying a second vogue and the sun pours in as you eat your bacon and eggs.

> 'I' plough the fields and scatt-er
> The good seed on the land. . . .

It's a good hymn; at least I always enjoyed it, singing the scatt-er bit and the way one's voice had to go down, down, down, went in fact with 'the good seed on' to ground.

I'd like to sing hymns again.

That's nonsense of course.

Yes I would, the rousing rollicker kind. I'd like to be there on Sundays in church with the rest of the village. They aren't; they're Chapel. There aren't any church-bells either. Lord how I miss church-bells! And bell-ringing practice on Thursdays, fading, floating over the garden wall, over the larkspur and lilies and red mascaraed poppies. . . .

You didn't go to church on Sundays then.

No, I didn't and don't go for those county/commuterbelt hats which pile into the dear old Norman church. At least the church here is hideous, and properly so, plain as a pike-staff,

8

thread-bare down to its yellow varnished pews. As to why I don't help to fill these, it's a complex and delicate matter: how profane, self-indulgent can you be?

One can't, I can't, attend for the sake of that marvellous-terrible organ, that marvellous-terrible locally known as rich – astonishing voice of Jessie Jilks, issuing from a face as ecstatic as a slab of uncooked dough; and the chat as you walk down the path that leadeth unto life, unto roast beef and Yorkshire. . . . For oh yes they do. And think of it!

I do think – of Jo, in her sixties still farming alone at Sleights, who on Sundays leaves off walling, downs her rake and puts away her grinding physical labour with quiet hands as if she were folding away her needlework. Oh for cross-stitch! Oh for Yorkshire pudding and peace of mind, for the crisp, clean, toasted soapsud smell of ironing!

You don't get round to much ironing.

No, I don't get round to much. . . .

But how I enjoy those Monday washing-lines, those terrible sugar-pink sheets that can't fail to clash and have never failed me yet on any line, never fail to wallop madly in the gale with the pea-greens and the lilacs and the long-johns.

But you don't enjoy doing washing.

No, it bores me stiff.

You think it's a waste of time.

Yes I do. I said washing-lines not washing.

Well don't you enjoy your own washing-line? No, for years you were so well-bred you had to get the steps and take it down every time you washed.

Look, I don't have a washing-machine; I do it in the bath. And I don't have sugar-pink or pea-green sheets. I have white sheets and bath towels that show every mark, men's Marks & Spencer shirts, socks, pants. And the last time I hung these out the cows ate the lot. Those cows owe me £60.

Washing bores you. Housework kills you.

9

Well, isn't it a kill-joy? Try scrubbing a hundred and fifty square feet of flags.

You wanted flags. You'd still want flags in any house you moved to. You bought those awful Ideal Home brass beds.

Yes, three beds for half-a-crown and, as such, ideal not modish. Everyone, including the auctioneer – 'Any old iron? Is Mrs Gore here?' – everyone thought I was mad. Everyone said carefully, 'How amusing!' Then (ten years later) 'Jess is so clever! She ought to have been an interior decorator.'

Well, I was mad. And we are not amused, Brasso in hand and the last tin I bought the price of six brass beds in 1952. Definitely not amused with outside, under the fells, three fields I've never seen before spreadeagled like a huge white aeroplane, the body and two wings yoked by that fat black outline the art mistress wouldn't allow, or not in my day.

Why are the fields white and the moor, which is higher, grey?

Why do you want to know?

I don't know.

But I know that I want quite desperately to walk along the lane and see once more, discover if the plantains and that desiccated marsh grass are still white with blossom, some like spiraea, others heavy with roses. And not just to see but to report; to enter: 'Today along the lane plantains feathered with snow like white spiraea; marsh grass heavy with roses.'

And why again? What is the point of your precious winter garden? What at least is the point of writing about it? No one wants to read of such things. They'd have to see it themselves. Each man his own winter garden.

That's true. That's how I'd feel myself.

But, how you depress me: why do I write? 'Why does Ma have to write?' wail the despairing voices of my children. 'Can you be quiet a moment, love?' said I to my son, aged six, 'I'm

10

trying to think.' 'I HATE it when you think.' 'Granny's forgotten my birthday again.' 'Granny does forget. She's working awfully hard on a book at the moment.' 'She's always been working awfully hard so she must be awfully rich. So why does she send such mouldy Christmas presents?'

I outline my new novel (the one I'm trying to write and can't, which is why at the moment I'm scribbling here). I say that the theme is a woman facing grief and age. An impatient frown appears on my sister's face:

'But people don't want to read about that! They want to read about love.'

I say that surely grief is a part of love. I am wrong: there is nothing to say about grief except get on with it. The same goes for age, life after fifty, when you've still a third of the way to go, the worst third – but no:

'For heaven's sake! There's enough *real* unhappiness in the world, goodness knows, without reading about it!'

I think we were both taught deportment but not the facts of life.

I think the Empire really does die hard. And I'm not suggesting you won't need that stiff upper lip. Merely that when I go out in the snow and the dark to the deep-freeze what I want in my hand is a torch not the rose of youth.

There is, after all, a thing called literature.

But since my sister will not turn to this, I shall disguise my grief-guilt theme as one of paranoia dished up in that good old rustic setting.

And to youth I, too, shall say gather ye rosebuds while ye may. I shall not put a placard on the cover: Keep Out, this is a book for the halt, the lame and the blind. For this would not only be fatal (forbidden fruit). 'We are the halt and the lame', they would cry, limping to the library on finding that I am not in paperback; bounding along in their track-suits en route for the Health Food Store, vitamin B for despair, and comfrey ointment. There's nothing like comfrey for Cupid's dart in your Achilles' heel. And I say yes indeed that arrow is painful. But bunions are worse. They do not believe I know about the dart; and they do not hear when I say that bunions are worse since no arrow will now alight, pierce and relieve me of that excrescence. Looking sourly over my spectacles, I say they should wait for bunions: I say that the book is out. I say they should look under Youthful Egotism.

'Queens have died young and fair. . . .'. 'I say,' one of them says afterwards, 'you know that old trout in the library? She said 'Queens. . . .' How they laugh! And how I wish they would – laugh more and give the wheatgerm oil a break.

'Well, Ma, why don't you get off your bum and write a book that sells, go to Paris, go to the Greek islands; come to London and stay with us – that's what we'd really like. Then we could go away ourselves. Charlotte needs a let-up.' Oh I know. I feel so guilty. . . .

Well why don't you . . . (write the Book that Sells)? Rubbish. Of course you could . . . standing on your head.

But I did try. . . . Don't you remember?

Don't we all. The shrieks of self-pity resounded from Land's End to John o'Groats.

So you see – it only made things worse.

Look, you rate low on household chores. You think they're a waste of time. Well, you could buy a washing-machine, spin-drier, electric scrubber, new vacuum cleaner; move house; lead a Normal Life. Try living for a change and learning to enjoy it. For Chrissake! And you ask why we're depressed!

Am I the cause, the whole cause? No, I have not that privilege.

But you don't exactly sizzle with sweetness and light.

Light. When I consider how my light is spent.

Well you certainly consider it. Take a long hard look (that's what I'm trying to do) and learn to burn the candle at both ends. There are two.

Ends and means. . . . For me there is only one.

In short the talent which is death to hide?

Yes, to me it's death.

Come off it, Mrs Milton. Washing-lines and moaning about flagged floors, love-hate for flags, hardly amounts you know to a *Paradise Lost*.

To me it does, oh, but to me it does.

For you have to be quick to catch it here, the patches of iridescence racing as cloud shadows race over the hills, spun sugar made of sunlight mixed with drifting snow, passing the line of butts now, skimming the walls; now leaping the trees which blur by the beck like fur, like a fox fur, silver fox; now rolling out of sight.

To return to the subject.

I can't. I'm taking time off here and I can tell you it's paradise regained. But my novel *is* paradise lost; and not just lost to my heroine.

In short, you prefer spun sugar? Yes and no. Sugar is what my sister wants, not that she'd much want mine. I, too, was fed, spoon-fed sugar for years. And it hasn't left me sweet. In fact it was sugar that put me in paradise lost. I'm still there, still trying to get the glucose out of my system, not having learnt to suppress the saccharine smile which still, for some reason, soils my lips down in the home-sweet-home counties which they certainly aren't to me.

So here I am on my mountain, not writing the Book that Sells, not wanting to give others stones for bread, wanting to tell the truth and nothing but the truth, which of course you say can't be done; which will be mine own and nothing but mine own convenient truth. What I need is the manure of life. And what good do I do in fact and how I do depress you. And well, aren't you a raging insomniac?

Yes, I'm having trouble. I can't write narrative. This is linked with wanting to tell the truth. I can't mate the two. But let us go carefully here. A little truth goes a long way. In this I'd agree with my sister: let us not . . . admit impediments. I am nevertheless, I am bound to admit, impeded.

'To begin to think is to begin to be undermined' says Camus, who is not however saying what my sister thinks; who also says, 'One will never be sufficiently surprised that everyone lives as if no one "knew"'.

Also – I could do with a few more *aperçus* and this perhaps may be a healthy sign, at least a suggestion that I am en route for a cleaner, leaner diet and on the path that leads to Lermontov. Clear concepts cleanly written. Where was I? Oh yes. Also:

'It was previously a question of finding out whether or not life had a meaning to be lived. It now becomes clear that it will be lived all the better if it has no meaning.'

That ought to set me up narrative-wise. And it does, in a way, set me up. But when I spoke of wanting to tell the truth and nothing but, I didn't mean The Truth or A Meaning. I, too, think life will be lived all the better without a meaning, that one is better off with the thing itself.

With bunions? Yes with bunions.

With age, cancer, grief?

I take it you're talking about reality.

Could someone dial 999? 'There's a lady who's cut her wrist here. Cut, not slashed . . . slashing the double-glazing. Could you send at once to remove this? It's urgent. *She can't see out*. . . . Yes, an acute case of condensation.'

14

'Dear Mrs Jones. Your frost-flowers have come. I've put them in the window. I can't tell you how grateful I am. . . . PS. I see you ask about flagged floors. . . .'

Well here I'm bound to concede a Meaning might come in handy. But I won't toe the sacramental line, won't offer up my flags unto the Lord. If I offer them up to anyone, the person who most deserves them is my patient, ever-loving husband.

I shall now, however, shut up about flags, also narrative. For I, too, am actually sick of my own voice. And thus begin to see the point – of those deadly factual statements, yards and yards of wooden paling fence which I laboured to erect and behind which I sat with outside (and in) all fluid, all flowing and changing?

Flaubert sat it out. I can't sit it out. You don't understand. *I haven't time.*

That's all. But while on the subject of death (well we are, you must have snoozed off) we will end with one more original apothegm which I'm positive I preserved for posterity somewhere. I rather think on the lid of a small blue box, which a fortnight ago still held a string of cultured pearls now reposing at Messrs Dibden. Yes, here we are:

'Washing soda. Brasso. Ring about Charlotte. . . .' No, no, try the other side. I do:

'N.B. That the narrative form derives only from death. Our one sure knowledge – that we have an end.'

Expanded, this would read roughly as follows:

'A man acquires an obituary – "a life story" – only after death. Before this he may possibly, and only, possess an inner pattern to which he alone has access.' The rest, as far as I'm concerned, is silence.

A deathly hush in which I hear the art mistress say not only are there no black lines in nature, but no straight ones either, taking away my ruler. But not in time to take away my foolscap.

15

Foolscap. That's perfect. How did it get called foolscap? Reach for *Pocket Oxford Dictionary* which says, just listen to this, 'Dunce's conical paper hat (Hist.), this as watermark of paper'.

2

Walking, at first, in a photograph. Then, against the snow, sheep near to, their fleece *camel-coloured*, in brand new 'horse-rugs', complete down to the stable-mark, the letter S clear and very red.

All one's palette, in short, wholly disorientated. Walking in a new unknown country. What, yet again? Yes, once again. Impossible to account for the fascination of one particular section of glacial patch-work patterns, very high; I supposed on Karva.

On Baldi Hill the walls; that beautiful long top wall patently enjoying its Cresta Run. All trees leafless and London black; or all but one, the rowan below Lobb's House, which, though bare and berry-less, remains for some reason russet, smouldering in the late cold afternoon.

The straight blue smoke of my chimney – blue, doubtless in retrospect – let's say the smoke of my chimney gave me pleasure. For as I kick off my gumboots I hear a sound as improbable in this house as the song of a canary. I half rush, half hope – for what? Some wild kermesse, the news that all the world is young and gay.

My heart, in fact, is heading for my boots (gumboot socks) as I pick up the receiver armed to hear, in response to my 'Hallo', a dubious 'Doll?' As usual a wrong number. Everyone is ringing someone else. Everyone here has dozens of people to ring – for pence not pounds, without the clockwork lady who says coolly, politely, 'Lines from Leeds are engaged. Please try later.'

I can still remember one voice, warm, laughing, confiding, and how I longed to say 'Oh, don't ring off! Talk to me, tell me why you are laughing, tell me why you are happy. Tell me anything, but don't ring off.'

Usually, it must be said, it's as I sit wrapped in my rug, complete at last with shooting mittens, hot bottle, pen, spectacles – these last having finally been run to earth, for which read linen-cupboard/clothes peg-basket, by the P.E. (Patient Ever-loving husband); generally it's as I sit mummified in my rug, the foolscap littered over my knees in a state which might seem occult to some but is not occult to me, that my life-line peals, peeling off my rug, scattering my foolscap. I pelt. The P.E., too, peels and pelts and will one day break his neck on that olde worlde spiral staircase. It is not, I need hardly say, Lady Bloomsbury-Bloggs, ringing to ask if we are, by any chance, free to dine on the 21st when Professor Galbraith will be staying. Nor, more to the point, is it *The New Yorker* panting to ask – well obviously nothing. It's the man about the logs: is the lane clear of snow, as he could deliver this afternoon?

This time, however, my heart abruptly deserts my gumboot socks: will I accept a transfer-charge call? It's Mark:

'Can I possibly come home?'

'Of course you can. When do you want to come?'

'Now. I'll leave now. But are you really sure, Ma? I know you're getting a novel off the ground.'

Of course I'm sure.

'It's just that Lucia and I are having such awful rows, I simply can't work.'

'Oh love, I'm sorry!' (eight weeks till he hands in his thesis).

'I'll be with you by 6.30.'

No, no. It's a good two hours from York.

What can I give him for dinner? The usual maternal reaction, loathed by one's children and to be heavily sat on. Fuss, the

18

great barrier reef. But when I go for an omelette with Alice, I don't see an omelette or Alice – she's locked with the Wok, oysters and bamboo shoots. It's a mystery – no, it must be fear, however deeply buried; fear that I have nothing to offer my child. Nothing but food. And in Alice's case? Yes, in Alice's case, too, I think it's fear, if for different reasons.

Is it Mark or Giles who can't eat eggs, red meat, butter or cheese?

What are we having? Fricassee of chicken, one piece of frozen chicken. Extract another piece from deep-freeze. See there are plenty of bacon rolls; and croutons – croutons for anguish. But I tell you he will – they all – arrive starved. The first thing, or almost the first, they say is: 'A slab of bread would do, Ma.' And then yes, they would like a glass of wine. They would like, he will need, a bottle tonight. There were, are two in the outhouse. *Chambré.* Make up the fire with infinite care. It still smokes. Nothing will stop that blasted fire smoking, and not only smoking. Smuts the size of gnats swan through the stratosphere idly pondering where they will finally settle. Meanwhile shovel foolscap into a case. Pat cushions, smooth divan, DUST, and draw the curtains – thinking as I do so how I love these, my red and white quilts, the striped one and the one with a diamond pattern; thinking of clowns and Picasso, and how they need washing and starching but how there is never a day and how heavy they are. Thinking 'not everyone has gentians in his house'; and seeing my son, as I've so often seen him, lying back in his chair, his face drawn, exhausted, murmuring 'Oh Ma, it's so marvellous here!'

Later the P.E. comes downstairs and I stop cutting the croutons to listen, as we always and fittingly listen, with holy dread to the forecast: a rapid thaw. Widespread fog. FOG. Some icy patches on roads. I've heard enough and return to slashing the croutons. The P.E. says this means that M. may well be late. I seize a skewer and stab the bacon rolls.

19

'Can't you come and sit down?'

'No!' I shout wrathfully. 'Of course I can't. The chicken's not on yet. . . !'

'". . . you fool!"' the P.E. finishes my sentence for me, laughing. But the cold catches my breath: he's gone outside. Returning, he says there's no trace of fog:

'Come out and see for yourself.'

I do. I see the pointed stars.

'Well, sit down and smoke a cigarette. I think I'll put on some music. . . .'

'If you don't mind. . . !' I snap.

We sit and discuss the Lucia situation. I sympathize with Lucia who is twenty, witty, *normal*, a knock-out and would like to go to parties – and does not share my son's obsession with Galileo and Kepler, or his imperative need to perfect each sentence. Mark, as we know, will make no further reference to Cupid's darts, nor by nine does the subject interest me. The only one which does is, is there any whisky?

The P.E. anticipates my need; and says: 'You know this has happened before. Don't you remember the time you'd got dinner ready for eight and at 8.30 Giles rang from London to say they were just leaving?'

And I say yes, Giles but never Mark.

I am wrong. At 9.10 he rings to say he isn't coming. 'I'm terribly sorry I didn't ring before.' He doesn't say that when it came to the point he felt a cad and that since then they've been at it hammer and tongs, for four hours. He says, briefly, things have been patched up; but could he come for the night on Saturday? 'You mean both of you?' No, Lucia is going to a party. It's two years since I've seen my son alone.

Writing in haste, for at any time now it will be light – *is* light enough to see the snow has GONE. The field below me is black,

20

streaked like a panther with white. Oh this whiteness! Nothing was ever so white. But already the black is betraying that it intends to be green, a very dark, waterlogged green. The flanks of the opposite side of the dale faintly scribbled in chalk. I have let my coffee get stone cold.

Curious that one should feel such a thrill at seeing the snow go when I'd so wanted Mark to see my Fabergé larches, ancient and matted but yesterday great nests of filigree silver, exactly like the gilt filigree nest with its opaline Easter egg which I use as a paper-weight but which once, presumably, held some knick-knack from Cartier's. As to why I preserve this *objet d'art*, it's a kick in the pants to the Empire, exuding at times a whiff of pure wickedness, like patchouli. This is the genie escaping from the casket in the shape of my great-great-grandfather, who neatly covered his tracks by giving his mistress a diamond necklace and his wife its duplicate – in paste.

The truth is I can't tear my eyes from sheep moving and grazing. It's an age since anything lived or moved here. Including your narrative? Well yes, I'm utterly stuck. Outside the house, too, it's a quagmire. But even from here, from the stile in the wall, I hear the roar of waters. The beck is in spate and where in the broken-backed South with its concrete lily-pools, no not in the grounds of Caserta could you find such primeval wrath of waters, such boiling of broth, such cataracts and cascades; not admittedly crystalline – the colour of onion soup. My bath this morning, too, was like onion soup. It's peat that accounts for the colour. The bowels of the earth are unleashed and if you find that unsavoury it's too bad.

Nowhere, meanwhile, not in Marienbad, is there mud to equal this and not just mud, a fishing net of mud, rings of slimy clay inches deep in water left by the hulking lunging Charolais. Immured now in byres, their spoor remains and walking is a nightmare. I nevertheless enjoy mud *qua* mud. A childish taste

21

no doubt, and self-defeating: condemned to watch my step and manoeuvre along the walls, I see nothing.

This is no great loss – there's nothing to see. The dale is as grey, dank, dull as could be. What, nothing to see? No; and what's more, *what's worse* is, if there were, I shouldn't see it. I should walk in my head, arranging and re-arranging the sentences, impounded behind the wooden paling fence.

I thus not only enjoy my mud, I am indebted to it. Not only does it remove my power to look, to see and fail to see and thus puts paid to despair, which puts paid to everything else, as the P.E. says – mountaineering in mud requires all my concentration, and I do not give a thought to the paling fence.

Mark says the trouble is Proust, Proust and *The Cherry Orchard*. And I say yes of course the trouble is Proust. But Chekhov is still Chekhov and might not Chekhov help – to clear away those rigid wooden stakes?

But Mark says no this is not what he meant and this is not the time, meaning or partly meaning after the shrieks, echoes of which are still, he says, picked up at Land's End.

'You can't put yourself inside fresh characters – yet.'

My answer is I've got them all lined up. And Lord, how they bore me!

'Then write something else. You can write anything you like.'

This is P.E. talk. I look at my Viking son and think this is the P.E. young again, blonder but with the same high cheekbones, the same 'criminal' ears (the first thing I looked for in his cradle), a face like a faun, the same wide-set, cornflower, strict, blue eyes which filled me with such quaking and tearing love. But this is not what I meant. They are mentally closer now: 'How's my ole man?' Mark says, wanting to know. And then they are at it and I am as out of my

22

depth as ever I was. Mark is the P.E. without the War. But he too and already is arthritic with writer's cramp, and knows you can't write anything you like.

He is, in fact, merely replying as I murmur weakly: 'If I could only do it in the first person. . . .'

'Well, what's to stop you? You don't have to be omniscient.'

'I thought I ought to . . . I thought it would be a corrective. . . .'

Not now, he says: 'Not when you're selling your *Cherry Orchard*, Ma.'

For yes, my frost flowers go on the market in June. The grief novel must wait, he says; it sounds like a major effort. And, crossing the fields that are yellow after the snow, washed out and yellow against the Prussian blue of the fells, he says:

'You know you'll never find anywhere like this.'

On our return we sit – Mark too, or so it seems to me – extinguished by my silence and exhaustion. As usual the late night has caught up on me. As usual. Can't I take one late night spent jawing with my son? No, eight hours' oblivion is vital to me. And why, have you ever asked yourself why? I don't need to ask. It's all there in the 'Ode to a Nightingale'. Including *The Cherry Orchard*? Above all *The Cherry Orchard*. Including the fact that I finally and as usual succeed in boring/failing my child to the point where he abruptly, indecisively leaves – before lunch.

As we walked he said: 'What you need at the moment, Ma, is an ego-trip.'

No, no!

'What's wrong with an ego-trip?'

'Everything,' said I, professionally, passionately, the Empire fairly oozing out of my heels, but still without foreseeing how the phrase would turn and rend me. 'Everything. It's the antithesis of art. And jargon to start with. And verbally repulsive. And. . . .'

'Cool it,' said the Viking, 'cool it, Ma.'

'Well, why can't you just say self-indulgence is good for you at times?'

As he failed to reply my eyes, following his, came to rest on Helwith Edge, its stone turned to gauze. At last, looking his last, looking away, he said:

'You know what my ole man calls John Knox in the attic? I call it Aunt Louise in the bottom drawer.'

My sister sees herself somewhat differently placed. This, however, is not, or is only in part, Mark's point: Louise is on a super-ego trip.

Later, as we went out to his car, he paused to look back at the house. Above the roof the moor was charcoal black. Putting his arm round my shoulders he said what everyone says:

'I know it's hard. But you're right to make the break.'

Now, with his car receding, I damn well know I'm right; and can't wait for my dream-house – Cambridge semi, two up, two down plus mod cons, bay window neo-Ruskin. . . . You'd be surprised what ghastly good taste will do.

Brown with a white door. The two down knocked in one, French windows opening on to garden; old apple tree; old roses. Herbs! I can grow herbs! And just look under the lino in the basement. It's brick. It's the kitchen, the rustic one you eat in. A touch of likeness makes the whole row kin.

And kinship is my business. Bicycling to kinship. Lord, how I've missed bicycling! Well, naturally you can't here, you'd be pushing half the time. . . . But what wouldn't I give for that bicycle now. What wouldn't I give for pavements, faces – other people's. Bookshops; think of browsing in a bookshop. Well, they don't grow on trees here. It's twenty-five miles to the library, fifteen to a decent piece of cheese.

Imagine it – shops round the corner. If you've forgotten the saffron, it doesn't mean that you can't, after all, have paella. *You can go back for it.* If you've forgotten the tea you can get it tomorrow. It's not a national disaster. You weren't going to buy ten packets. You aren't going to be snowed in for six weeks.

For, lo, the winter is past. . . . The figtree putteth forth her green figs . . . and the voice of the turtle is heard in our land:

'The peas are nice and sweet today; fresh-picked this morning. . . .'

'And turnips, four pounds please.' No need to say white.

'Having a *navarin*, dear?'

'Well, yes, as a matter of fact. . . .'

She's partial to one herself. 'It makes a change.'

'Who, then, are we having to eat it? Nell, first of all Nell, who will always be first always being just Nell, small and wry and wise under her mouse-brown fringe, with whom one says to oneself 'Nothing too much'; but Nell knowing it all, love and the deserts of love – my touchstone of the truth and nothing but.

Sybil, on the other hand, is endeared to me by her tremor, and daring to wear hats – oh but beautiful hats, and carry these off with distinction. She will not, of course, wear one tonight, but tall, vulnerable, bird-like, will still be the Duchesse de Guermantes in my collection.

Ildred won't come, he never does. Who shall I sit her next to? The expert on Persian ceramics we met at Gertrude's. That leaves two married couples to put asunder. Firstly Hermione and Eric: Hermione (who has a new lover) witty and drawling, will have to seduce the P.E.. She will still have the new Professor of French. And Eric (who has an ulcer) will have the Professor's young wife who is *très aimable*.

New friends, new thoughts, a new self; a future not just the past where memory shakes a few, sad, last grey hairs. For even memorywise we are growing bald; thin on top, or I am, in every sense.

The attic's bare. That's rubbish. The actual attic's crammed, so jammed I can't face clearing and cleaning it out. And I can't expect the surveyors to pioneer through that lot, old curtains, the children's riding hats, tennis racquets, the basket for baby-powder and napkins now filled with dolls wrapped in that table-cloth – yellow shot-silk, fringed – from our first silk-damask drawing-room. All of which only proves my point: the attic's a lumber-room. I live in a lumber-room; and don't, it must be said, respond well when the P.E., chatting in bed, says: 'Do you remember that dish, painted with fruit, I bought you that time in Ely?'

Yes, of course I remember. And Ischia, the scirocco, everyone watching those evil yellow breakers, then everyone getting up and suddenly seeing it was Giles – *out there*, doing his best to drown himself. Of course I remember the children's dance when you rigged up that marvellous pavilion and that blossom, Gerald Bossom, knocked you down because you happened to mention that Alice had got into Newnham and his blossom, Henrietta, hadn't got in. . . .

But don't you see it's this that inspires my matutinal despair? Don't you see we're behaving like Darby and Joan? That looking forward can't be exchanged for looking back? Don't you see that we've ceased to accumulate?

We've never replaced that dish you bought in Ely for 1/6d.

Well yes, of course it got broken, like everything else. I've smashed a good deal in my time. Everything in this house is cracked or chipped, including yours faithfully.

Soon I'll be cracked beyond repair. And, in fact, seldom any longer risk an hour that once supplied our waking *persiflage*.

Though when I don't no less than when I do, when flinging

back the bed-clothes – death in my heart – I fling out of bed, I all but succeed in cracking the P.E. And when he's got galley proofs and deserves, if ever man did, to go to his study cherished and fortified, to be given back, in short, for once in his own coin and oxtail stewed with grapes in the evening. At the end of his day to sink down in the room with the drawn curtains, a room where the logs blaze and the shadows dance and I blaze the glad news abroad that dinner will be at eight (not ten and *à trois* with the clockwork lady from Leeds).

And he does not, does not deserve to wake to the brass bed bounding, resounding with for whom the bell tolls, it tolls for thee:

'Well, I've been up two whole hours. I couldn't find my pen and I still can't find my spectacles.'

The P.E. finds my spectacles, but even he can't find the short stories – two – I'm trying to write and had in my hand when someone rang and gave me someone's number. Anyway I used these to write it down. One was called *The Chest of Drawers* and the other *The Room in the Field*. I'm rather upset about *The Room in the Field*. I thought I was on to something there.

You thought you were on to something?

Yes, something I didn't understand.

You mean you didn't know what it was before you started to write? Simenon wrote a whole novel in six weeks. He mapped it all out and then went into retreat. Gide thought Simenon a master.

I know; but if you've worked it out what's the point of writing it down?

The point is prose, limpid impeccable prose.

No, the point is in the process. You need the photographer's dark-room; you have to go in there with your negatives, and that's what they are I can tell you. Lord how they negate, nag, niggle, refuse to cooperate. You have to take them in there and plunge them in the ink and gradually you will see the plate emerge, not in the words, beneath these, like trees reflected in water on one of those mute motionless winter days.

To return to the subject.

If you mean that impeccable prose, I can't.

I thought you were so hot on the thing itself. Well that's what a novel, what narrative is, a thing in itself *per se*. A statement. A canvas within a frame. It doesn't overlap the frame.

It didn't. It was in a frame; that's just it – framed in my window-frame.

And all right I've lost the story, but not the room in the field. Ever since I found this a week ago I've waited and each day now the wait is a little longer, already the days are actually lengthening out and I actually wait with impatience, with a mounting sense of drama for the moment when I will draw my red and white quilts. Or rather don't now draw these: leaning forward I ensure that the sheep are *in situ*. Bundled under my window, drawn by its brazier light, they look up at me still mechanically chewing gum.

And then it arrives – the room in the field, the sheep under the table, clustered among its ball and claw feet, around the pedestal which supports the marble top, and the amphora – behind me, as I stand, a washed out terracotta – shapelier now, a shape, one I seem to know but do not know. And there, out in the twilight, is the scrubbed Provençal sideboard; how long it has grown, how it stretches away. It's the angle. Yes, that explains it. I have always seen it *en face*. It's the same with the bust, my poor man's Verrocchio. Inscrutable in its child-reserve, a boy off the streets of Florence, how blandly it suffers itself to be transposed. Before, it has always looked through me; but now it is looking away into a room I know and do not know. It is true that the bookshelves are there in their place, on the wall at the back of the room, above the divan scattered with cushions and books. But not as I know them to be – dim, incorporeal they dream where I have never lain or been. In a room I have never entered. Is it simply this? Do I or do I not wish to enter that room? No, I wish simply to know it is there. Framed in my window pane? Perhaps. I don't know. I can't explain.

But it's obvious. You've always wanted, you'd still like to live in a barn.

No, no, it's not as simple as that. I don't want to *be* in the room in the field. And its strong point is I can't be. If I step back from the window it disappears.

And perhaps this explains my distinctly semi-detached obsession (no, with the Room in the Field), that it comes and goes; that in the last resort it is there, but also insubstantial. I should find it less substantial were it not so.

The pageant being insubstantial, all fluid, all flowing and changing? The wind's changed, the semi comes and goes. Change is in the wind.

No, *the wind's changed.*

> No! No! They can't
> Take that
> Away
> From me!

Oh bourgeois crying in the wilderness! There, here's your Chobham garden. There, there! Here's your concrete lily-pool.

3

I'd thought the problem was choice, alias indecision. No wonder you can't write, said I to myself. Poor little darling, of course you can't. You're rotten with vacillation. You can't even choose what clothes to put on in the morning.

So you cut it out and went into black for mourning – no, for morning.

But the page stayed as white as driven snow.

Driven snow isn't white. I know; it's driving now, flailing past level with the walls. Grey not white, it can't be white, the speed breaks the flakes. Driven snow is grey and bites like grit. So whoever thought up that one had snow like sex in the head.

I too have snow, but not like sex in the head.

My diary? For, yes, April 8th:

'Force myself to walk. Snow over my boots. My feet so cold I can't stand and look. Saw two things only: against the snow in the field above Lobb's House something like a patch of scrambled egg – on inspection a dead, newborn lamb with the after-birth red beside it. The lamb, however, not curled in a small limp ball – laid on its back with its legs up, frozen as it fell. At the top of the hill I encounter a single ewe. Even she has beat a retreat, repelled by that yellow pancake. An eerie hush. When does the cuckoo come? This is Never Never Land. Approaching my Wendy house, something makes me look up at our sycamore trees; something uncannily like an acute distaste. Each bough hatched black and white, they look like a wood-engraving. Yes, that explains it. I've always loathed wood-engravings.'

Well, it's hardly, you'll concede, an adequate adult diet.

But Jess, you used to rave about the winters. Don't you remember the first one when you hadn't a deep-freeze? You saw that flurry of snow in the field below, and realized it was a stoat going at and at a rabbit; and you rushed out and rescued the poor thing. It wasn't hurt, just mesmerized and you laid it on the doormat, thinking it would recover in the warmth. But it died of fright – in the nick of time – and gave you four square meals. . . .

Yes. I gave up that story years ago. Likewise the one about our rushing to each other's studies to say 'Look! Quick! There's a peewit in the field.'

A visitor, in short, in case you've missed the point.

Your diary, in other words, was no fuller then?

Not in the sense that yours is full, but in others fuller by far, if not as the pad by your telephone is filled – ordaining how you will spend today, tonight, tomorrow. My appointments were purely extempore.

Did I imagine, did I invent or merely collaborate with 'Snow creaming like surf, a diminutive breaker over the gap from Arkledale, then roses all the way. Snow hard and uneven as I walk. A wild streak of bird's egg blue in the sky above Winterings, and by midday the far side of the dale green halfway up, a dark unappetizing green. Here we're as crusty and white as ever we were.'

A first, fond, reckless rapture – from an early journal.

'Snow-flakes fizzing like flies, angry as bees.'

But these pleased me no less: real winters still existed here! Reality – it's still obtainable here! Well, Englishmen in the tropics dream of the changing seasons. It's the force that through our green fuse drives the flower – and drove through Beethoven, Kant, Rembrandt, you've only to list the names; all the names. When Federico of Urbino sent for Justus of Ghent he sent for the North. . . .

31

Winter – an undiscovered country! And what was more, more to my point, you had to learn the language. To do so you had only to report:

'Gold clouds. Gold river. Scrag Hill copper mauve.'

Copper and mauve?

No, *copper mauve*.

And now? Now you ask 'où sont les neiges d'antan?'

Yes; and it's not a rhetorical question. Were all those gay glad tidings that seemed a justification, my only justification, a pack of lies? No, they were true, I swear it. And now – the snow drives past grey like grit, level with the walls. We're 'fast in' as they say up here, we've been fast in for six weeks. Captivity is also reality.

Captivity is freedom from choice.

I didn't choose choice when I came here. I chose something obstinately external.

Nature is always a malleable feast. It's less demanding than friends.

Perhaps.

Now is the time, now is your chance – to fill an empty world, an empty page. . . .

They're not empty. Both are filled: we're five degrees below zero and can't afford to run the central heating.

So you can write narrative! Factual, pithy, clear. All you need is characters and a plot.

Passions spin the plot. Unfortunately in my case only an excruciating boredom; agonizing, humiliating, disproportionate effort. There are enough, there are too many books. What is the point? Well, what is the point of killing myself in order to kill time for someone in a train?

I thought you thought so highly of the art of fiction?

I do – far too highly for me to profane it.

Reading list: *Malone Dies*
                Hunger

The Last of the Mallous
The Lost Lady
A Book of Common Prayer

(Beckett, Hamsun, Simenon, Willa Cather, Didion.) Note the massive significance of the titles, to which I need hardly add *The Myth of Sisyphus* or *The Ballad of the Sad Café*.

Net result: they can; I can't. I can't even read. I read to filch, to steal, to learn a way.

So much for narrative. A fig for narrative. This is Pluto's land, zany-land. Here in this twilit underworld I owe, barely owe, to the sickly gleam of a 100 watt bulb, my spinal chord thinks it's Napoleon.

A rat's gnawing my shoulders.

They've amputated my feet.

They can't have done; you woke in the night with cramp.

No, in a cold sweat. That dust on the dining-room table: it's woodworm. *Woodworm* in the ceiling.

The place is riddled with rot.

Moths are eating the carpets.

They'll never get the outside painting done.

Come now, Jessie, just because you've noticed a bit of woodworm! And think what luck that you noticed it in time. All old houses have woodworm. In fact Charlotte's mother has the Rentokil people every year.

Rent-a-kill for cancer. Cancer of the stomach. No, not tea; the tannic makes me retch. Food, I'm obsessed by food.

But you have a proper breakfast?

Somehow I can't get out of bed in the morning. A hot bath? In that bathroom, with a damp towel? No thank you. And besides, by the time I get up I'm so desperately late. Late for what? To watch the snow flailing past like grit.

But you do have regular meals at regular hours?

33

Yes, hourly in fact. Dry toast with Bovril. An hour later toast and marmalade. An hour later – well I can't possibly wait for lunch. . . .

So at last you see, Jessica, what a mistake it is not to lead an active normal life.

Wives in Wimbledon windows gaily waving their dusters – he's off to the Stock Exchange – 'Bye darling! Take care! See you!' I should die of it I tell you.

Well isn't it better than your Swedish drill, *yours* – your spine, your feet, your cramp, the book you can't even write? So it's you you you that fills the page.

Yes, an immense shadow, like the elongated shadow mysteriously cast – when? – by our sycamore trees, five hundred yards to the foot of the field. At what time of year? When they're still bare; winter trees.

(Like Charlotte's legs when Alice gave her hashish in a cake and her legs stretched out as far as Brighton Pier.)

Well, there's nothing else here but my shadow at 5, 6, 8 a.m. Today looks as if it will never dawn; grey, lifeless. But more to come – snow piled in the sky; meanwhile possibly saying 'Pause, pause', as the Chopin said last night (Ballade in G flat minor) played more slowly than usual by a Russian. Only a whirlstorm, I thought then, could produce such distillation. But still I clutch my pen and maunder on. Why can't I learn to be still, to wait? Because I haven't a brain, or the confidence – only a pen instead of a mind; and the mad hope/belief that if I get down something the day will not have been entirely wasted.

Time wasting away. How fast the time runs out. The lives of the great always seem so long; which is why I can't read history. Lack of historical sense. History is time made permanent – which it is not. Lived time is NOW, a crystal stream rushing through my fingers; no, like cabbage water down the sink.

34

Sinks – how bored I get by reading lethal attacks on homosexual poets who pee in the sink. What does it matter if they're drunks, drug addicts, social snobs? The real sins are a failure to enjoy, to make something out of what lies to hand. Pettiness, spite, acedia, lack of lovingness are the only sins I understand (too well). I don't believe in the will much, it shouldn't be necessary; variety seems to me the better way, i.e. getting up when everyone else is asleep and you're outside the tedium of routine. Free! To recover the feeling of freedom of the spirit!

Failure. Fear of failure makes me fail.

And yet all this terror, this horror in the face of wasting time, how do I reconcile it with the waste in which I exult – the profusion of those beautiful double snow-drops round Lobb's House which no one sees but me. The heartsease, the whitlow grass, the small persistent harebell, the buttercups blued by an endlessly drifting rain – that these would be here without me, just as these hills and skies will roll on whether, wherever I am or am not, is precisely what constitutes their divinity for me. Birds so busy nesting – yet I myself loathe nesting, and nothing makes me so miserable as to be busy.

Naturally. If you're busy, you don't see the birds. As for the rest, the waste, the reckless waste – the heartsease that grows in its thousands but only in the Fallows, each looking up at you with a different face, for no reason, no reason at all, the harebell that grows in the loneliest stoniest places, grow for themselves by themselves, hinge on no effort of yours. No effort of yours could bring these into being.

The relief! The relief. At last I can down tools. I don't have to do it all myself.

And that is why you are desperate now. Desperate for 'otherness'.

Perhaps. But perhaps I've lost the gift for this. For a moment the blizzard lifts. But grateful as I am for the beauty of it, for a glimpse of the dale with its opal whites, opalescent rouge, I look sick at heart, sick at heart.

4

Once upon a time there was a young Canadian Mountie.

One day he fell off his horse and broke his neck.

He recovered but failed to regain the use of his right arm.

He took up painting.

He was rather good at this, not quite good enough but anyway he looked like a Greek god, and the long and short of it was, *the long and short of it* was that he ended up in Paris in 1920.

He wasn't an intellectual so everybody loved him, starting with Gertrude Stein and Sylvia Beach, which meant you were off or rather on with Picasso and Hemingway and practically anyone else you like to mention. So he had a lovely time in the *Closerie des Lilas* which is a fatal thing to have since an English pub isn't the same, isn't the same at all, and Nancy Cunard didn't know who he was. After the war (during which, being by this time bilingual, I rather think he answered the telephone in somewhere like Portsmouth in French) Paris wasn't the same. So he stayed and getting older wasn't the same. In fact from the age of forty you could say it was perfectly awful. So he took, on the strength of his spine, to using a cane, and by dint of this and the clothes he'd worn in Paris in 1920 looked enormously famous and distinguished. By dint of which he also contrived to stay in stately homes and so avoid financial/domestic problems. I forgot to say that he oozed charm, so that when at the end of three months this palled he could always ooze to other places.

Finally the day came when, deciding to write his memoirs,

he decided to tuck up for the winter here. The P.E. groaned, but I pointed out that he'd have his own bed/bath/study and a stove on which to cook his own breakfast. He didn't cook it. Each morning on the dot of half past nine, two hours after I had started work and was just getting under way, he appeared round the bend in the stairs in a flared and waisted mauve-blue dressing-gown (cravat to match) oozing charm, refreshed, fresh as a daisy, well let us say pomaded and over-cologned. And sniffing the mystic smell of coffee and bacon and eggs. Fragrant with hope. Today he would start to work.

And then? Well then, of course, it snowed. And snowed and snowed and snowed. And he lay on his bed all day with the curtains drawn, requiring breakfast in bed and feeling terribly ill. Terribly terribly ill until 6 p.m., when your host is clanking the ice in the martini, and you smell a heavenly smell of – it *must* be – *boeuf en daube*! The P.E. and I now jump when he enters the room. Can he have overheard our secret confabulations, our roars of wrath, our muffled yelps of pain, our groans 'What can we do, when will he go?'

At last, at last the snow-plough comes. I rush to the spare room: the lane's clear: 'Oh! You mean I can leave?' Yes, there's a train. . . . It's eleven o'clock.

He couldn't possibly be ready in time to catch the 3.15.

Well I can't possibly either – wait till tomorrow: 'Hallo! Could I order a taxi, please?'

For twopence I too now would spend the day on my bed with the curtains drawn: I too would murmur faintly 'You mean I can leave. . . ?' And decline to go. If you offered me London, Paris, Rome on a plate, a hot beach under the sun-burnt Sierra Nevada, I should close my eyes and murmur 'I couldn't possibly. . . .' All desire has withered at its source.

The snow-plough comes and we get out. I totter to the chemist.

'Just sign here', says the old crone behind the counter.

Sign? Where? Why? I gaze wildly at the prescription.

'Well, dearie, you're over sixty aren't you?'

Me? Over sixty? Over fifty's bad enough. I belt home and, like a stricken deer, blaze all the lights in the bedroom. It still isn't light enough. I take my hand-mirror to the window, or to be precise, crane with this out of the window. And there are ravines – five – on my upper lip. Two deep and hideous lines run from my nostrils into *dewlaps*. My chin looks like Queen Victoria's. How long is it since I bothered to look, look properly in a mirror? I suppose it's just been too dark to see.

But the next day it's too light. White snow-light fills the rooms. The P.E. thanks the Lord it's come at last, meaning the start of a thaw, the only pretty ring time. The P.E. hasn't a line on his upper lip.

I shall never forgive this house.

I shall never forgive this winter.

Well if you'd sat it out as the P.E. did, patiently, cheerfully restocking your mind, absorbed in the sack of Rome, you wouldn't look like the sack of Rome.

And why are you moving anyway? Because the Iceman Cometh. 'Pull down thy vanity', said Ezra Pound over and over and over again somewhere in the *Cantos*.

I can't; and dash off a letter to Hermione. I haven't seen Hermione for two years. We can't have people here without the central heating and Hermione's latest lover lives in Rome. Hermione laughs and doesn't believe about the ravines and dewlaps, and doesn't know anyone else who has these yet. That's just my point. It's too early to pull down my vanity. Hermione says she will find me a face-lift man.

The address is Harley Street; it sounds all right, but isn't. The waiting-room, identical with those where you wait for your deaf-aid or your death sentence, is filthy, littered with stubs and sweet-papers. Nor are those with whom I sit the well-oiled *crème de la crème*. But this is why the face-lift man is cheap, I tell myself eyeing the underfed, patently underpaid, scrawny girl who is patently not a model, eyeing the men – they are mostly men – seedy looking clerks. . . .

I am blinded, further blinded by what awaits me: the strip-lights, the whiteness. I might be in an operating theatre. And the surgeon, surgically dressed in white, does in fact cut me up. First of all he removes my right to speak. It is his, not my, decision what I have done to my face which, it appears, *is* almost past repair. He is thirtyish, thrusting, virile, and writes with his sleeves rolled up; forearms, hands covered with thick black hair. For twopence he'd punch my face to a jelly; no for £500. Weakly I sit in a chair under the arc lights. Photographs are taken. There are ten not five ravines. My dewlaps aren't; they look like the cliffs of Dover.

Out in the street I pull my scarf up over these like a yashmak. Pull up – no, pull down thy vanity. Haul up thy self-respect.

Bate, I beseech you widow Dido.
O, widow Dido; Ay, widow Dido.
Is not, sir, my doublet as fresh as the day I first wore it? I
    mean in a sort.
That 'sort' was well fished for.

Down with the top-mast! Yare! Lower, lower! Bring her to
    try with the main-course. [*A cry within*].

The top-sail's lowered. It couldn't be lower. How low can you sink? Full fathom five. Bring her to try with the main-course. No, not that; I can't. The head-wind's too strong. Tack. Tack

40

desperately up Harley Street. It's useless. We're aground. The vessel's sprung a leak. Keep right on to the end boys, Auden said.

The end. Till death do us part. How long can I count on, count on still having the P.E.? Two, four, ten years perhaps.

How can I steer that course, knowingly?

I can't. Without the P.E. nothing would keep me on course.

Haven't you learnt to stand on your own feet yet?

Apparently not. Does anyone stand on their own feet?

Yes. Some people manage it.

Not completely.

I can't leave this house. We've been too happy here. Happy? I was under the impression. . . . No, the wind's changed. *Change is in the wind.*

> No! No! They can't
> Take that
> Away
> From me!

5

Do you realize there is nothing, no books, no wisdom, no guidance to which a woman can turn when facing age, decay, grief? Of this women have left not a rack behind.

Jane Austen did us a poor service. Her old women are all fools. She has no more time for them, bereft of beauty and youth, than had Montaigne.

In the last resort she funked it. Why? Because she was a spinster. Because malice cannot, without bad taste, be made to run in harness with age, suffering, grief.

Will not a male testament suffice? (I am, after all, no longer a woman but a 'person'. I have been raised to the ranks of a human being.)

Montaigne, then, for example: 'Every example limps', he says as if to send me about my business. Books he found useless to him, no guidance possible since no two beings live, love or suffer alike. 'They had better catch the pox themselves if they want to know how to treat it' is Montaigne's medicine, not only for physicians. 'For every foot its own shoe. . . . Its pursuits have no bounds or rules. Its food is wonder, search and ambiguity.'

There's a man at the door. He says you want the double-glazing back. I did. But I don't after all. Could he take it away?

I want. 'I wanna banana *now!*' says my grandson Jamie.

No, 'Could I have a banana, Granny, please?'

Please could I simply sit in the window watching my pearl-grey larches stirring, bathing, laving themselves in the rain.

They alone jut, tilt.

Everything else has gone missing. All else, if silence were a colour, mute.

But no, I must go to Wimbledon or Charlotte and Giles will divorce. And it's my fault. I should have gone before. When I arrive they are both out, at their respective shrinks. For Giles, too, I find is on the couch. Giles who doesn't take after me, but after the P.E.! No, Giles rides himself with too tight a rein. The shrink, what's more, has shrunk him so tightly he hardly utters. I feel shut out, childishly shut out – and in pain, as, a bag of bones, he downs his third whisky. At last, at last the children are in bed. But why don't they clear up their own toys? Because there are far too many and too elaborate. Charlotte clears these up; beautiful, talented Charlotte, haggard and drawn, who, sinking down in the chaos, tells me that things are no longer the same between herself and Giles: that Giles is on the 'phone till four in the morning, doing business with the Arabs, doing nothing, wanting to do nothing but work. Needing the cash in other words, but not for all those toys. For a bottle of whisky a day now, Charlotte says. Charlotte herself works at the Academy of Music. And I think, think with pain of her wedding day, of waking to the ripple of her Cimabue fingers playing what? The music of pure joy. Of Charlotte's miserable childhood, thrown out by her rent-a-kill mother and locked up with a governess across the park. And then she found Giles, my locked-up lonely Giles. And wept in the

43

church with incredulity. At last they had found each other and now they have lost each other. Charlotte believes that Giles no longer loves her. I say that this isn't true. I know it isn't true. But Charlotte weeps. She is almost too tired to care.

In the morning she shouts at the children. Giles shouts back. They depart for separate destinations.

Jamie weeps. The baby bawls. The au pair sits in her room; they are playing 'Night and day you are the one'. No, I am the one. It's time for school: 'Here's your satchel, love.' Andrew says nothing. He picks up the other satchel.

Bicycling to school he wobbles ahead of me, literally to and fro across the road. It's sheer devilry. No, it's hate. No, it's the death-wish. I am afraid for Andrew, afraid, afraid.

Andrew is living in torment. He's old enough to know. But I am deprived of my grandmother's rights/rites. I cannot spoil, cannot get through, cannot redeem my role as the unwanted intruder, the hated one. I cannot say 'Guess what's for lunch? Fried fish and Queen of Puddings!' They each choose what they want when they want it. They've never tossed a pancake or had Lemon Meringue Pie – only the agonies of choice. Agonies? Come, the menu's confined to the deep-freeze: 'I wan' ice-cream! I wan' fish-fingers now!'

The baby wants its bottle now. I want my spectacles. How much milk-powder did Charlotte say?

I want what my Mummy gives me. You shall have it, my love, you shall have it. And this evening I'll show you how to make calendars on which you can cross off the days. No, that's negative. Tomorrow I'll think of something; a better way.

Meanwhile this evening, 'Andrew, Jamie, Mummy is going to ring you.' I want to say 'Will you promise me something? You're big boys and you don't want to make Mummy unhappy do you? Promise you won't tell her you want her back. Mummy's very tired. She needs a holiday.'

I've no right to tell them what to say.

They are waiting, bathed and cherubic, in their dressing-gowns.

Andrew tells Charlotte he wants her back. Charlotte wheedles, appeals, bribes for twenty minutes. She'll bring him a lovely present. No, it's a secret.

Jamie says 'I wan' you' over and over again. Monotonously. In a stubborn monotone.

I take the receiver from him before Charlotte shouts. I say 'Naturally. . . . But we're shaking down.'

Jamie's too young. He's worse than Andrew. Andrew will go off the rails. But Jamie will be a thug; he will bash his way out.

Out of extremity. They are both in extremity. Oh my children, my little ones what can I do?

What have I done? I let Giles be miserable at school. The P.E. didn't want to take him away. He said Giles would be unhappy at first wherever he went. We tried and tried to get him into a day-school; and got Mark in but not Giles. Are all prep school masters phoney sadists?

It's no good going into all that. What can I do now?

Get off that mountain and into a semi. Fast.

Meanwhile I still haven't finished clearing up the nursery. Which is part of which construction kit? Why do they have them all out? By ten o'clock I know. My grandsons are like Penelope. This is their tapestry. Each day they toil – at the destruction of construction kits.

I can't unravel this tapestry.

It's not yours to unravel, says Alice.

Alice thinks it's my tapestry.

The next day the au pair washes and irons, is Swiss, in love, slimming. In my diet, too, fish-fingers are *verboten*. I eye her salami and salad pointedly and successfully. She departs for her school and to drop Jamie at play-school.

Andrew is back and wants nothing, nothing that I can offer. Naturally. Besides which it's hot. Lord it's hot. Naturally. It isn't in the Pennines. All I need in one of Charlotte's tee-shirts is mint, no caper sauce. We'll have no more of that. What you need is a canopy for the pram. Andrew finds the canopy and fixes it on when I can't. Woman, woman how low can you sink? I don't care, it works. It's the first thing that's worked. And now into the car with the carry-cot. Collect Jamie, and off to broad beans, iceberg lettuce, new potatoes, mint, *haricots verts*! Baby carrots – carrots in bunches with their leaves on!

'What are those for, Granny?'

'For me to eat.'

Tongues round ice-lollies, like calves licking salt, two pairs of solemn eyes digest the shock.

The worst part, the worst part I'm beginning to think is the dog. If only it wasn't for that incessant yapping as, locked in a ball, the boys roll fighting down the stairs. This is the worst, the fighting and yapping hour; Pippa the dog's favourite hour as she races to and fro – yap, yap – she's forgotten the puppies. Four, which are seizing the moment to squirm under the fence and out on to the road, *on to the road*.

If I thread bamboo through the chicken-wire and then staple it down, that might do the trick. What sort of staples?

What sort of staple will staple me down to this for twelve more days? The knowledge that it's only for twelve days.

But not for Charlotte, not for Giles. No staple will serve me there. No staple will serve to fence that knowledge off.

Worse than being old, ugly and old, is the fact that being old you are useless. To them you are useless *because* you are old.

It's as if they're professionals. Pros. I did an amateur job.

How do you do a professional job?

I thought you did it by loving, wrapping them in a bath-towel and singing Here we go round the Mulberry Bush. And Snakes and Ladders and mumps and turning their pillows over and reading *Brer Rabbit* and *Tom Sawyer*. But finish your first helping first, and in bed by seven; you'll catch it if you get out again: this is P.E. time.

Yes, and then? Still loving, and camping in the rain; and Alice snooty and smouldering in the car reading 'How to be a Success at a Party' in *Peg's Paper*. And trying like mad to look right for her half term; and the P.E. crawling around my hem with his mouth full of pins, and Alice saying I always had holes in my stockings. Loving and keeping one's ear to the ground and not always enjoying. But enjoying it in sunny Italy when the P.E. took Alice out and gave her an ice-cream and told her to sit on the beach as she sat on a sofa.

I still thought you did it by loving. I thought there was something called fun. And then? They woke up going round the Mulberry Bush, woke up going round and round on a cold and frosty morning.

I admit I didn't go round that Mulberry Bush.

But they chose it, oh yes they did. And then they got hurt; and tough. Even Mark? Yes, Mark is paternal to me.

They're having their revenge. At last they're top-dog. It's the old old adolescent story. But they're not adolescent. And there's always a mulberry bush. And I am not simply the head au pair.

It's as if they had access to some esoteric knowledge which has only recently come to light. On sale in the Health Food Store for under thirties only. But Alice is thirty-four, thirty-four.

Alice is tough. She has to be, in the Corridors of Power; the VIPs think she's the secretary.

Tough and dicky as hell; in short, the mixture as before. Sip

47

through a straw, with extreme care.

Don't be natural, it might wound. Don't relax, you're naïve. I thought you *liked* me to be embarrassing.

Well, would you rather I'd taken, took lovers and smoked pot? No, this is their very own private hell.

But marriage is a mulberry bush and not all a merry-go-round. You go round and round being two instead of one. And it's a thing you do go round, saying to yourself how could I? I'll never be alone, ALONE again. It's a shock to your solo system when you're used to going to bed with ten of the books you'd got from the London Library (because you couldn't be sure which one you'd feel like reading) and your mother put her head round the door and said 'I can't think why you want ten books on the bed'; and now your husband says the same thing, *and* takes them off the bed and you think 'I'll never read Kant' – and the next thing is there's Alice and Giles and Mark.

And you never do read Kant.

It wouldn't help Giles or Charlotte if you had.

Rubbish. That's Louise talk. Louise can't Kant or doesn't, but she'd lap up the *Critique of Pure Reason*. Kant, like Louise, thought better of 'objects of will' than 'objects of knowledge'; and came, I am sorry to say, by devious means to a sticky end, the sticky end which is where Louise got stuck: 'Only that which is done solely for duty is moral'.

Stick with the thing-in-itself, say I, and keep your hands clean. And watch your epistemology.

All the same Kant did say something en route, when he got, so to speak, on the train and before he got out at the other end as God, and Moses was on the platform and Kant said 'here it is – the Categorical Imperative'.

Before that he said the object of knowledge was experience, experience of 'natural, causal connections'. This led you to

48

reflect on the relation of ends and means which led to 'dexterity' and 'counsels of prudence'.

I'd go along with that, assuming that by dexterity Kant meant something less slippery than it sounds. I wouldn't give prudence the time of day. But consider that Sophocles would and did, consider its role as conceived by the Greek chorus; and you think again.

The fact remains: I can't honestly say that my experience has borne the fruits it surely should have done. And don't think I haven't tried to winkle these out. Don't think I haven't carted it off to the Fallows and up Scragg Hill, reflected, dissected, connected, wheedled, warned.

But once the wind rises experience avails me nothing. Once Prospero conjures Ariel:

> Hast thou, spirit,
> Performed to point the tempest that I bade thee?

my reflections are no better than confetti.

> Rock-a-bye baby on the tree top.
> When the wind blows the cradle will rock.
> When the bough breaks the cradle will fall
> And down will come baby, cradle and all.

Well, you'll admit it's odd, an odd lullaby. Do you think it's vindictive? Or just true?

I once asked the P.E., and he said 'No, it's comfort. It's saying they'll be all right when the cradle falls.'

But they aren't; they don't drift down on a breeze in a rain of apple-blossom. They don't land softly in the summer grass.

They crash, they land with a thud. And say 'You hung the cradle there. You ought to have known, you knew that bough would break.'

Yes, I told you the truth then and I'd tell you the truth now.

What truth? I must know something that would help.

'Jesting Pilate, asking, "What is truth?"' says Carlyle, 'had not the smallest chance to ascertain it.'

No, but he didn't ask in jest. And truth *is* a way and a life. That's all. Being as truthful as you can.

But what is the point of everyone going round the mulberry bush, round and round since the beginning of time?

What is the point, my point if I can't help Charlotte and Giles?

The point is that Louise would put them right. And it wouldn't help.

No.

That is the point, your point. Hold it. Stop wanting to help, and be.

Meanwhile the au pair washes and irons and says, what is 'eatwave? She 'ave 'eard this word on radio. I too 'ave 'eard this word, though strictly on radio. I explain that the sky is blue, the weather is hot: 'Oh no, we 'ave always this weather since I come I think.'

A heatwave! I can't believe my luck.

I find the paddling pool and the thing to pump it up with. It won't. There's a hole, no three holes.

Bicycle tyre repair kit. There must be a bicycle shop. Find it. Pull down thy vanity. I can't. Ingenious, dauntless, proud I patch and fill the pool, and Andrew is actually in it: 'I'll splash you, Granny!' Actually dancing and laughing. This is my finest hour. In fact it lasts for exactly ten minutes. I fetch Jamie from play-school and change the baby's napkin while Jamie knifes, knifes the paddling pool.

And you send him straight to bed. No, it's hotter in the garden. I merely hide the knives, all the knives. And wonder

50

how the heck I'll get through the weekend. We could go to the sea. Perhaps we could go to the sea.

Meanwhile you read them *The Wind in the Willows*? No, they watch telly. I think I need someone to read me Henry James.

No, what I need is someone to give me the glad eye. In that case I need the P.E. No one else. Quite. Well, what more do I want? Nothing. And it happens to be true.

All the same. . . . Yes?

It's not the same for men. Age shall not wither them nor custom stale their infinite variety/opportunity.

No Women's Lib can lib you from the fact that they're still in mint sauce when you're in caper sauce. No equal pay, no high-powered career can save you from the fact that you're still alive alive-o but the male doesn't caper with cadavers; and, genetically speaking, I'm sorry to say, for impeccable reasons.

Face it; and go out to dinner with Jason.

Perhaps. I'd much rather wander round the Tate, sit on the tube, look at other lives. Lord, what wouldn't I give to swan along a pavement. In this heat? Besides you're on duty.

And your duty is to let Andrew stay up for dinner one night, and Jamie another; and let them toss for it.

Jamie wins the toss. Menu: fried fish, new potatoes, fresh peas, fresh fruit salad. Eaten in silence, but eaten. The hostess sweating blood: 'What's your school like? What do you like doing best?'

What is going on in that child's mind?

That he wants to ask a question, and doesn't know how or what he wants to ask. Jamie is Hercules bashing the Hydra, bashing, labouring, grappling with the monster of an amorphous question.

51

Help him. How? Sit on the floor and play Beggar-my-neighbour.

Jamie shouts: 'I won! I beat you, Granny!'

A break-through! Tonight, at least, the Hydra will skulk in its lair. One night isn't enough. It's a start. Chalk it up. Chalk it up that you're almost half-way through. Almost? I'm not *even* half-way. . . .

I'll never be through.

So she [Alice in Wonderland] went back to the table, half hoping she might find another key on it, or at any rate a book of rules for shutting people up like telescopes: this time she found a little bottle on it ('which certainly was not here before', said Alice) and round its neck a paper label, with the words 'DRINK ME' beautifully printed on it in large letters.

And then? Well, then in the morning she had an awful headache and the lawn looked like a slab of toasted cheese. Water it. What's the point? Well what *is* the point of a lawn in Wimbledon?

What's the point of going nuts in Wimbledon Jacobean? Meaning it's more pointful in the Pennines?

It's wet and cold up there; in fact sleeting the P.E. says.

They'll never get that outside painting done.

> Hierusalem, my happy home,
> When shall I come to Thee?
> When shall my sorrows have an end,
> Thy joys when shall I see?

Tomorrow week. And perhaps I'll see Giles, and Charlotte, happy and well. Meanwhile, face it; go out to dinner with Jason.

6

Once upon a time. . . . Once upon a time – well, it's fairly obvious – there was Jason, looking like Dylan Thomas, Dylan Thomas young – soigné and impeccably correct. Also in uniform, rich and spoilt. When Jason came on leave Scott Fitzgerald wrote in person and said 'There shall be no Blackout', and you walked along the streets with London glittering like a Christmas tree.

And it wasn't just the chandeliers and champagne in buckets which were what you were walking to with Jason, or the matchlessly soigné decorum with which he clicked his heels and bowed to his infatuated hostess. It was Jason soigné and clicking, bowing out of the ball and whisking you off to the Hammersmith Palais de Danse; or stealing a boat and rowing you out on the Thames off Cheyne Walk and both of you wading, pushing the boat back in, Jason tripping over a chain which gave an almighty clang, Jason letting out a shout of laughter, and you dragging him up the steps and both running for your lives, and dripping into breakfast at the Ritz.

Dripping into finnan haddock and Spengler and William James and Browning and *The Brothers Karamazov* – and what the P.E. thought about Yeats and said about John Stuart Mill; and the hopeless things the P.E. did: how he couldn't find his rifle and fell asleep on parade; until, of course, he was sent on a night patrol, which was a tactical error or perhaps a tactful way of getting him out of the way and winning the war.

It was Jason who introduced us; in the London Library. Somehow I wobbled to the Ritz where the champagne tilted in my glass at the sea-sickening angle you only see on deck in a Force 9 gale.

Jason was best man, is Giles's godfather and still sees Giles. I thought he might help about Giles. Jason has given up marriage but is faithful to the Ritz, though when you arrive he isn't there. You sit on the dais and wait and wait until you decide to leave, and then, as you're stepping out of the main door, you see him just inside this, sitting hunched in a chair, so hunched and deep in a book he's invisible. When he isn't reading it's worse; he's hunched in an awful coat, lost in the limbo of despair – until he sees you, and leaps to his feet flinging out his arms, rescued, radiant, young and Savile Row.

I suppose there are plenty of people who would find this distasteful, contemptible and painfully obvious: the glitter of the show has palled for the poor little rich boy. But the point with Jason is that it hasn't palled. His marriages palled. Yes, because nothing else did; of course he was incorrigibly unfaithful. In other words selfish and weak? Yes, if it's weak to be married for money, play the fool and repent at leisure. He wasn't always married for money; Celia was rich in her own right – but fancied the Embassy in Paris. And whipped him out of linguistics and into politics, which two matters cannot be made to mix. So one fine election day Jason disappeared, I rather think with a lady up his sleeve. Anyway he didn't surface until the divorce was through, when he sniffed the air, scurried home from Yale, and there he was in All Souls with, up his sleeve, a book called *Liberties of Speech*.

In this learned work – it's above my head, I quote the P.E. – Jason contended that language is on the way out, cannot get its tongue round a scientific equation, and will shortly be a burnt-out case. Soon we shall indeed lisp in numbers. Only the charlady, clutching a few Shakes-phe-hearian rags, will be left to gabble in gobbledegook.

The omnivorous British public fell upon Jason's warning as

if it were the Pope's Easter message, or Wittgenstein's *Tractatus* transmitted by Barbara Cartland.

So he tootles you off to whatever is whatever *l'Étoile* was, and it's like walking in with Jonathan Miller? He enjoys the tinsel of the show? Yes, and isn't it better – better than turning martyr, than togging yourself out in sack-cloth and ashes?

Jason likes damask napkins, dresses in Savile Row, is formal, fastidious, suffers from personal charm; also from despair. In seeking to salvage language, he thinks he has only hastened its demise.

This said, let it be said that no *bon mots* plop between us over our asparagus and sole. Jason's talk is three-parts asking and listening.

Tonight he asks first and as always what the P.E. is up to, and then what I am up to in Wimbledon.

By this time I no longer believe that Wimbledon exists. But Jason says I am wrong; it's near Putney. People play tennis there. And I say, you don't read the papers. It's the place where grandmothers cut their throats. But it's miles and miles away, on a Desert Island Disc.

'In that case there must be palms. . . ?'

No palms. I tell him about the paddling pool.

I intend him to laugh, and he does. The same thing still happens. Everyone in the restaurant suddenly looks as if they're on the verge of remembering something they've dreamt. The dream goes back under. They go on eating.

By this time, looking at Jason, you'd say that he'd never laughed in his life as I tell him about Giles, Charlotte and Giles. Crumbling his bread he listens with sober, acute intentness. When Jason listens it's something you can hear. Occasionally asking, making no comment, finally falling silent, he does not immediately offer to see Giles.

Instead he asks what I'm writing. I say that I am not. I tell him about the wooden paling fence, also 'obituaries'. He's crumbling his bread again. It's my turn now to ask what he's working on.

Glumly he says, the same thing. Then suddenly he's off, off where we were when all the world was young. Off on to Dostoevsky:

'I forget the words, but something to this effect: "That the causes of human action are invariably immeasurably more complex than our subsequent explanations of them."'

All right, but I wasn't born yesterday. Wait, he's saying something, something about Giles; yes Charlotte and Giles. Something that will help. But no he is not:

'At times the best course for a writer is to confine himself to a simple narrative of events.'

The restaurant goes up in smoke and descends in smithereens. Somewhere in the debris the voice goes on:

'And this is the line we will adopt in giving an account of the rest of the present catastrophe.'

No, this is the last gnomic straw. All academics are mad. They can't even light a panatella. This simple human feat achieved, Jason, my one-time friend, sits back and leaves the narrative to me: meaning, I snort, one that implies all that Dostoevsky knew and condenses all that Dostoevsky says.

Jason sits blowing smoke-rings and doodling on the menu.

Suddenly there are waiters with damask napkins flicking imaginary specks from pointedly empty tables.

As we stand, about to step out of the lighted door, Jason looking through this is seeing – the Swanee River? No, the Styx; it's the same thing.

But we've always been looking into the Styx.

It's flowing faster now. Faster and blacker.

Now we are on the brink.

Living and leaving. Living is leaving. We can't be leaving yet. Piero della Francesca's 'Death of Adam'. The faces of

Adam's children. Their bewilderment. Yes, that is how youth looks at death.

By Adam came death. . . . But Piero's Adam was old, older than old, terrifyingly old.

Jason is young. He will always be young, as young as Adam's children.

The look on his face isn't bewilderment.

The death-look. It's gone now, as I slip my arm through his and we set off back to where I've left the car. As I am getting into this I'm surprised, I'd forgotten – but Jason hasn't. He says he will see Giles.

It's two in the morning. And Wimbledon is miles and miles away, has definitely moved to a Desert Island Disc.

At last I'm there, flinging my handbag on the bed. Something falls out on to the bed. The menu. Jason has slipped the menu into my bag. There's something scribbled at the top:

1. That it is, of course, easier to explain than to refrain.
2. That the writer's function is to help, let others find out for themselves. Anything else is tantamount to advice.
   Advice from your humble servant,
   Jason.

7

I'm back – and off the hook.

Yes, back *at last* with a book on your hands, and we're panting to hear what happened to Charlotte and Giles. And Alice needs expanding. You must have seen Alice in London.

Yes. Alice ruined that day at the sea.

Why?

You're not going to hear. I've done what I had to do, and that's enough. I don't have to write about it. 'But,' peering over my shoulder, breathing down my neck, you say, 'just when we were almost giving up, after flicking through page after page of nothing but sheep and snow, just when we were getting interested – well faintly, if not exactly sold on the subject of grandchildren, but when you were starting, it seemed, to see the light/get the knack, you throw it away.'

Yes, that's correct. I'm not, quite frankly, hooked on the subject either. I take your point, Jason's point, but when I take it up, the setting won't be Wimbledon Jacobean. One further point, Lermontov's – as distilled in Bowra's preface – his 'detached, self-sufficient art':

Lermontov, who, as a soldier was brave to the point of recklessness, never thought that the life of action mattered except as material to be turned into words. [*Nota bene* 'turned into words'.] In this he was helped by being exiled to the Caucasus, that stupendous land of mountains and rivers. . . .

Well I'm back in my Caucasus, and what's more, myself exiled, thrown out by Andrew and Jamie, *thrown out by Charlotte*. A happy release? No. I don't want to think about it. I was going to leave the next day anyway. Later perhaps I'll see it was funny, funny and perfectly natural with Charlotte and Giles both back; and as jumpy as cats. Eyeing each other. Back and *out*:

'Well why not,' I'd said to Charlotte, 'try it, suggest it?'

And all right I had turfed them out (for a pub lunch together). And it does, can do, had, I could have sworn it, done the trick, or started to, when Charlotte walked in radiant.

Intrigued, I thought by the silence, surprised, as I hoped relieved, that she hadn't been met by two tear-stained outraged figures, in retrospect hurt, perhaps, that they hadn't heard the door, as, engrossed, they watched me podding those dashed broad beans (they'd never seen beans in pods; I wish I'd never seen beans) and stroking the silk insides of the green ears.

Still radiant, I thought, as if in a trance, she'd sat down, picked up a bean and was starting to tell me about lunch when Andrew must have seized a broom, Jamie the squeezy mop and one each side they drove the message home: 'Get out! Mummy's here. She's never gone away, never gone out with Dad like this before, but as long as you're around anything may happen. How can we know that she won't vanish for good?'

Poor little loves? Later perhaps. But a metal squeezy mop is definitely first cousin to an axe. Damage apart, shattered and shocked, leaping up I said 'Oh Andrew, oh Jamie, how could you be so horrid?'

And Charlotte, Charlotte of all people, actually only said: 'How dare you criticize my children!'

Giles – almost the worst part – simply fading out. . . . No, that was better, that was right. He was tacitly siding with Charlotte, and isn't that what you went for?

59

Isn't that something to chalk up?

Later perhaps. Today, thank heavens, I've other uses for chalk. First the bullocks – a curious meeting, greeting: all, when I went downstairs this morning, my first morning back, and drew the curtains, *there* outside the window, not my delicate, black and white shy Nigerian ladies but huge hulks of beef with huge bull faces. And every one, worst the creamy Charolais, covered with mud. Why? Well, it's muddy. Yes but they don't roll in it. It was like drawing the curtains and finding a herd of hippos looking in.

And then – well then the rain, glorious bucketing rain, the rapture of hauling on my gumboots, and off. Succulence, wetness, oh Lord, it's marvellous. I'm parched – and soaked; and drinking, drinking it in. In fact by the time I reach our gate it's already drawing off, and I'm startled when a workman in a pick-up, coming over the top from Rigg, hurtles past, then stops. Even he is astonished by the sight: now I know why the farms climbed so unsuitably into the snowlands. The whole flat floor of the valley is a delta – no, paved with formal oblong shapes and squares of slate-grey water. Above and all around, odder still, the whitest of white mist throwing the hills about. Which hill is which? That can't be Baldi Hill, always bald, always blue, its crisp clean denim profile washed each night and ironed in place each morning – falling about now, falling apart, and with all that scrub, *scrub* – or is it rocks? – tumbling down. It must be Baldi Hill, but if it's Baldi Hill it's drunk and it hasn't shaved for weeks.

The whole of the opposite side of the dale channelled with silver streams, new becks I've never seen before.

Dazzled and dazed I head for home. 'Home is where one starts from'. With your words as my only compass, Mr Eliot, also the sudden thought that their context may be still more

60

pertinent, impelled to hasten back and look this up, I climb the hill. It's not I who've lost my bearings. Our own house is adrift, afloat in the whiteness of mist. The sycamore trees, too, have cast anchor.

House, where are you going?

Woman, haven't you seen, heard what the elders, the mountains, are saying up there?

And the waters prevailed exceedingly . . . and all the high hills that were under the whole heaven, were covered.

I don't have to move house. My house is doing it for me. Wait, my Noah's ark, I'm coming too.

'It was not (to start again) what one had expected.' Mr Eliot, you're better than I thought. Where, you now ask, and where indeed, lies the

> Long hoped for calm, the autumnal serenity
> And the wisdom of age? Had they deceived us,
> Or deceived themselves, the quiet-voiced elders,
> Bequeathing us merely a receipt for deceit?

> . . . . . .

> The wisdom only the knowledge of dead secrets
> Useless in the darkness into which they peered
> Or from which they turned their eyes. . . .

Yes, this is the bit. Back in my seat by the window with the bright rain blowing past, I read, read on. This is the bit I need.

> . . . There is, it seems to us,
> At best, only a limited value
> In the knowledge derived from experience.

The knowledge imposes a pattern, and falsifies,
For the pattern is new every moment
And every moment is a new and shocking
Valuation of all we have been.

. . . . . .

In the middle, not only in the middle of the way
But all the way, in a dark wood. . . .

Exodus (Wimbledon Chapter and Verse). Back to my bare
hills, back to quietness and calm, to the P.E. I think 'that fills
the bill, and not just for me: for Andrew and Jamie, for
Charlotte and Giles. For Alice? Yes. Even Louise. For Alice
and Louise the wood's too dark.'

As I think this it occurs to me that there's something wrong
somewhere, that it doesn't fill the bill for the P.E. Thrown out
I'm forced to rethink, a process in fact confined to thoughtfully
plucking a thread from my threadbare skirt. Well, reading, as
has been said, will serve in place of thinking. (And, if you've
missed out on Schopenhauer going to town on this fallacy as
embodied in Pliny the Elder, this will sort out your adrenalin.)

So, passing the buck, I pick up the book, flick through, can't
find the place, and at length give up at the wrong, no the right
page:

. . . And do not call it fixity
Where past and future are gathered.

I don't. One can't. But you did say, Mr Eliot. . . . I read on
and don't like the smell of it. I think I smell fixity. Spare me
your preaching, poet. I'm off to the beck.

62

Off – and in mid-May still ahead of the spring up here, as usual delayed by the sleet and only now, in a biting north wind and only in nooks and crannies, tentatively starting to unpack. Rowans extending small, identical, perfectly fluted fans. Hokusai. A gaggle of geisha girls. And copper, bright copper magnolia buds that in a week or so will somehow turn themselves into sycamore leaves. Inspiring a hefty thought for the day? No, to look you must fold away thought. To see is the cure for thought, the cure for grief. Sycamore buds will serve, suspending past and future, to suspend you in the moment, the here and now.

Suspended, the roar of the beck, too, sluicing my mind away, I fail, I suppose, to hear the patter of rain. It gets dark early here. No, there's a storm brewing. It's time to go home and hear the P.E.'s news.

The flood news first – and it's brutal. The river after the sleet was already, of course, as the P.E. explains, high. And then came sun, a blue sky starting to melt the snow, the men all away at Rigg (market day). And then at the head of the dale the blue sky turning black. Racing over those tourist waterfalls, the river came down so fast, Rose Rash said afterwards, folk in Helwith hadn't time to ring. Cattle drowned in byres, chained rams swirled round trees, old Agnes Pepper's car washed away. . . . 'You'll have to go and see Agnes,' 'Of course I'll go to see Rose.' Reality – it's still obtainable here.

'Meanwhile. . . ?' I ask mechanically, or rather start to ask, still seeing those rams and not just rams, the ewes – brought down to lamb and some which had; mentally still seeing Tom at the foot of the field, head down, breasting the blizzard, Rose, too, ploughing through snow, plunging through drifts – day in, day out, *day-long*. Fighting the fight it takes here. . . . And old Jo Hurst at Sleights, low down, hit worst of all, the P.E. says.

I don't want to hear any more, and don't as he pokes the fire.

Straightening up, happily scanning my face, he smiles a questioning smile.

Sorry, what?

Cheerfully he says it will keep, and proceeds to answer the question I'd started, intended to ask, left unasked: how has his work gone? He's finished his sixth chapter. His sixth! He can't have done. . . . Of course I'm pleased. Pleased and utterly happy to be peeling parsnips and swedes. Meanwhile he's not been idle in other ways. That rising damp by the rag-box isn't; he's found a man who found a hairline crack in the copper pipe. Weather permitting they'll definitely start the outside painting on Monday. He's also (also been waiting for me to see, is waiting now for the look on my face) had a chimney doctor, and the fire *is* – drawing like a dream!

The logs blaze, the shadows dance and the smuts, no, sparks fly upwards as, blissfully rising to draw my red and white quilts, I ask, fittingly, gratefully, ask how he came by this miracle man.

Suzette had heard there was someone in Scab – Suzette! Alias the Wrecker. The Wrecker's back! And in trouble with smoke (since when?). So they tootle off for the day, have lunch in the pub, find the man, look at the church. . . .

Tootle off for the day and have lunch in a pub. Wild horses won't drag the P.E. out of his study with me for the day. Wild horses? Well no, perhaps. Subtler methods.

Listen, he did it for you. Then naturally tootled her home, and when pressed to pronounce on her Beaujolais (*nouveau*, in fact as fresh from Paris as is the Wrecker herself, who if she can't pronounce on her native product, can't in her native tongue ask any man on the pavement – Rue des Saints Pères – *can* ask the Baron de Rothschild to do so for her).

This bracket seems to have bulged. Skip it, bearing in mind the need in future to break up your sentences. You try to pack too much in.

But I can't contain my feelings.

These are precisely what you will have to contain. As a woman, *as a writer*, and not in a platitude. And no more tootling. This is journalese.

Also obvious, not to say trite; not to say perfectly normal; and childish, unworthy of you, unmerited.

Yes.

Well, come – after plonk the Beaujolais is nectar. It's absurd to go home and eat an egg alone when the Wrecker has olives, pâté and cheese, youth, beauty and brains, literary fame (albeit a temporary hang-up), knew Bunuel, knows Braudel, and still knowing Braudel, wants to know about *The Sack of Rome*. Of course, it's flattering. And the P.E. says as much. After all he's being perfectly open with you: is openness itself.

Yes, wide open.

When was that chimney actually fixed? The following day? Well hardly! But ten days later.

He isn't being open with me.

If I'd been out to stay with Hermione in Rome I think I could bear it better. What's eating me is that blasted paddling pool. In other words, that I've nothing comparable to offer, comparable with youth, beauty, Braudel.

I can't compete. No, it's pointless.

No, don't stoop to compete. You have something to offer, something better.

Such as what?

The way you will now behave. To start with, being pleased and showing it, that he's not been unhappy and lonely.

The strength I will bring like a rabbit out of a hat? Strength through joy, no through pride. Insouciance. Laissez-faire. Give her some rope and the Wrecker will hang herself.

But she's done it before, and he always forgets. He's

65

forgotten about last year. . . .

Forget it and whistle while you work.

Brasso, scrub, whistle. The P.E. does forget, goes out to buy and forgets his own cigarettes; puts his head in *The Sack*, forgets the telephone bill, forgets that the 'For Sale' sign will go up in June. No, he's trying to pay the bills and working against time. And isn't it better, the better way? The only way to be happy, pay bills, get books written? Write and you will whistle while you work.

Now is the time, now is your chance. . . . Later will be too late. The day will come when there'll be no moving house. No rope by which you can hang yourself. Well, haven't you much in common?

Yes, we have much in common, the Wrecker and I.

8

I have less in common with Rose, less than I'd like to have.
Rose has made a difficult man happy, a dark man with grooves
in his face, silent, highly-strung, and not, as Rose says
laughing, 'built for cauld': thin as string, the worrying kind,
with two lads and not enough land. It's not an uncommon
story here. Nor are happy marriages. 'The farmer wants a
wife' isn't simply an old children's song; and isn't, you'll
notice, about the baker, the tailor or candlestick-maker.
There's plenty of what comes of that in Rigg. When a farmer
wants a wife it's to shear and share alike, to bake but also milk,
muck in, muck out. It's a case of pulling together, and you can't
where there's trouble and strife; and don't bounce out of bed
with death in your heart. You bounce out when the alarm goes
– fast, dog-tired from yesterday – and half awake make a cup
of tea.

I have, though, seen Rose depressed. She didn't come out
with it; but I thought, and said I thought, it was there in her
voice. I'd been asking about their Christmas, and she said 'I
dawn't knaw; but somehow I couldn't seem to enjoy it this
year.'

The boys were what now? Fifteen and sixteen?

She'd never heard of that sinking Christmas feeling? She'd
found it for herself and didn't down or deny it:

'Ye knaw I've niver been that waie before. But I couldn't do
nowt about it.' And it lasted for a fortnight. A fortnight.
That's what I like about Rose.

Or one of the things. . . .

One where I'd go along with Schopenhauer – whom I picture, as we set off now, laying about him to right and left at the nettles, at those people who reject anything which threatens their 'preconceived notions', whose 'crotchets, whims, fancies . . . at last become fixed ideas'. This comes of being raised on 'books alone', in place of being 'made acquainted, step by step, with *things*'. Is your journey really necessary?

Well, that's what they used to say in the war.

Meaning, by 'really necessary', vital? Yes, to me it's vital to go down the hill and see Rose. And first see her washing line. It's not Monday. On Rose's line it's every day; and still today going like a galleon in full rig with its pink and pea-green sails, and crying to the heart 'Ahoy there!' crying 'Alive alive-o' – when you're hanging them out with your fingers stiff with cold? And bringing them in, when you're tired, to iron? And doing it every day? You think there's life in those sails, life for Rose?

Yes, Rose's life, lived life, today perhaps a life-line. And eyeing her over the rim of my Nescafé – hair cropped like a gamin, eyes bright as sloes – she's better, a great deal better than I expect.

We sit at the kitchen-table: 'Ye'll not maind? It's warmer is kitchen.' Mine's like an ice-house. Lord, what I'd give for that Rayburn! 'And saw cheap to run! But, bye, it's hot in summer.' This isn't, though, what she's saying now, stirring her coffee; is saying – no, exclaiming, 'Storm was terrible! Saw sudden laike, wi' naw time to bide; and wanting dogs. They're raight dogs as'll always cum, but there I was in yard stood hollering; I felt a proper fool. Then it caime to me: where's darkest plaice? It'll niver be cawl shed surely. But when I looked in shed that's where they were, laid shivering and panting, fair flayt wi' fright; and I thought I'll have a raight do getting 'em out.'

'But you did?'

'Na,' she laughed, 'they near knocked me down, bolted through door like as they'd niver cum back!'

'So what did you do?'

'Well, I thought best was down under. For lambs, ye knaw, with ewes behaving like daft. Ye'll maind they'll not like wet and gaw for wall, will sheep. But bye, you'd have thought you were watching potato raice!'

'And the lambs couldn't keep up.'

'Nay, they were little 'uns; they'd not be more than three or four daies old. Though we'd wun lot awlder, twins; they nigh brawke m' arms.'

'You don't mean you carried them all up.'

'Oh aye, two at taime.'

Ten lambs and five journeys. Up that hill:

'And that brought mothers, ye see, and that wi' dogs fetched rest.' She got them all in.

'You must be proud.'

'Well, I'll saie this, I've been wet before, but I reckon if Tom ud cum in he'd uv put me in bucket and down drain.'

And the cattle? All safe. All, of course, in that big new white top byre.

They've been lucky she says, luckier than most.

'Most' is a difficult concept here, and one which I don't explore.

As Rose herself would say, 'It's complicaited,' thus tactfully disposing of 'it' as merely a family tree the ramifications of which make that of Jesse look about as useful, chaste and ornamental as an espaliered peach on a north wall.

And family life (there's no other kind here) is certainly complicated, not to say, as any solicitor knows, nasty, brutish and short when it comes to dividing the spoils. The trouble with Rose and Tom is that they aren't – sufficiently complicated, corrupt, on the council, in other words in with the Mafia of the dale.

All the same I don't tell Rose that I'm going to see Agnes Pepper, don't know why I can't, and shall never know why Agnes is treated as she is by her own son, Jacob, and is now, rumour has it, to be turned out – out of the house in which she was born and into a council house. You might as well put Agnes in the ground – as off the land she farmed for sixteen years alone after her husband was gored to death by the bull: Agnes, left with three bairns, one of whom died of croup, and who handed over her capital, the farm and all she had to Jacob when he married, and then worked on as an unpaid labourer. Unpaid and unconsulted. If you ask how they've done at the market, her answer is 'Ye'll have to ask m' son.'

But you don't ask Jacob anything, with his round, red honest face. He can't, he tells me, afford to throw money away and won't, on that account, be at the Harvest Barn Dance – and isn't. He's at the tables in Monte Carlo.

How do I know if he doesn't say? Precisely because it's a secret, and if there's a secret the dale will ferret this out.

Agnes's position lacks the status of a secret, and inspires neither interest nor compassion. So that I didn't have to ferret it out – that she hadn't, as I could only suppose, played the matriarch and run the farm over Jacob's head. Jacob was spoilt to death. So how does one puzzle it out that still, at seventy-eight, mucking in, milking and hay-timing, the place where I will find her isn't in the front room by the fire?

Picking my way down the old stone track – where six hundred feet below, the cow parsley, feathering its leaves, will soon, already perhaps, tomorrow, lavish its lace; bluebells, flinging into the fields beyond, fuse blue with green (no picture-postcard bluebell carpets here); primroses gently claim their place in the sun on the top of banks lapidary with campion and herb Robert; the water-avens hangs its strawberry head – I don't go as far as the foot of this but turn through a wicket gate which leads past the back of the house to the old stables.

And, yes, she is there in her loose-box – the only place in the house, her own, which is unchanged and where she feels at home? Isn't in other words, under Judith's, her daughter-in-law's feet? But here the mystery becomes impenetrable. Jacob is one of the Mafia, Judith a quiet woman, old-fashioned, unhurried, plump, freckled, plain, keeping hens and not unlike one of her own Light Sussex, keeping a pig for bacon, making cheese, churning her own butter – kept, it's said, 'very short' by Jacob, but happy and somehow making that marriage work.

But not – out of loyalty to Jacob? – making Agnes happy? Wisely, where Jacob's dealings are concerned, keeping her thoughts to herself? And putting her marriage first – keeping those of Agnes at a distance?

Yes, perhaps, and perhaps in a loose-box. But in a council house? You might as well try to fit in Karva itself.

And it's not just her physical stature as she looms now in the loose-box, as usual looking out through binoculars; it's all that's implied in the face she swings towards me, slowly, without surprise, a beam in her eye.

There's a largeness in Agnes, a grandeur, wisdom, appetite for life – I suppose the word is humanity. And if this concept doesn't find you as it leaves me in the pink (which, this, too, being late lamented usage, it possibly may not do) look it up in Fielding and I don't mean ring the RSPCA.

You think I'm being condescending? Well that's what Louise would do, what the *crème de la crème* have always done and what, at this very minute, they're doing in Broadcasting House to judge by the clangers they drop when they read the news.

So all I'm saying is watch it, or that splendid old richly encrusted barnacle, the tongue Fielding wagged, will soon be as *maigre* as – without the precision, elegance, subtle taste-buds of – the one on ice in the Institut de France.

And I'd challenge Balzac himself to encompass Agnes in that *sorbet*, as we sit now each on a milking stool.

'So you're after a swim?' she says.

No, I've come about the car.

'I doubt ye'll be as good swimmer as car. Swum as far as bridge, did car.'

'In that case won't it do as a motor-boat?' I propound the idea that what is needed here are canoes and snow-shoes. After all they manage in the Rockies.

'And how'll ye git sheep up rapids to Rigg?' she asks. 'Na. Ye knaw what we did in old days – walk. Walk sheep over, men and all knitting as ye'd gaw. And sleep by roadside; bye, it was grand, was that!'

'In the snow?'

'Nay, you'd a fire, and folks ud sit around talking. And you'll not git talk rushing round in car. And not knaw folks the waie ye did when they'd walk ten miles to see yer, and ten miles back, and ud cum for daie.'

All the same, she'll replace the car?

'Na, what would I want wi' car?'

I wait. Does she mean that she won't on the housing estate? You don't ask questions here, but in the end I risk it:

'Agnes, it's not true that you're moving out?'

'So you've heard that tale?'

'You mean it isn't true?'

She leans her big face close to mine: 'Aye, it's true what ye've heard, and likely heard it before I did meself. Ye knaw where I got it? In garage when I went about car. "So you're moving out, Agnes." "What's that?" I sez. "Put yourself down for bungalow." She chuckles, rubbing her thigh. "And wangled yerself to top o' list" he sez. Agnes, I thought, ye've made it at last; they've put yer top o' list. I couldn't keep from

72

laughing all waie home. And ye'll not beat this – for a' they knaw I knaw they've still said nowt!'

She sits back triumphant, luxuriously sharing the joke, savouring this, crossing her legs in their breeches and thick ribbed socks, her amusement as rich as rich fruit cake. Enjoying it, actually enjoying the situation.

'But' – I'm bewildered – 'you don't mean you'll really go?'

'Na. Our'll gaw,' she says contemptuously.

She can't. A *bungalow*.

'Dinna fash yersell. I'll bide a bit. Till they've fettled east wing.'

I laugh, but don't think this as funny as Agnes does.

'Listen, I'm going to a better plaice.'

She doesn't think it better any more than I do. Despite this I can't help nervously eyeing the rafters. Hooks. Halters. *Rope.* Rubbish, that's not in her style. I'm on the verge of laughing at the thought of Agnes fumbling to fit her great face through the loop. But don't laugh: cancer. It's hopeless. A matter of weeks.

And, yes, she's leaning forward again now, dropping her voice low: 'Ye'll not tell? There's not a soul as knaws.'

Apart from the doctor presumably.

'Well, I'm going where I'm wanted.' Going to a nephew who farms in Appledale.

My relief is huge. But Appledale – I don't even know where it is.

'And there's none as will,' she says with infinite relish.

'You mean you'll do a bolt?'

She doesn't know the expression: 'Na, I'll not be for bolting. I'll taike m' taime.'

As she says this I have the sensation of hearing the actual chimes of a clock fading somewhere in the distance. Or the gong, perhaps, which, in my childhood, rhythmically pounded, resounded, sending, still sending out its ripples of bronze to those who, with my mother, now sauntered in from the garden and repaired to repair upstairs at their dressing-tables; my grandmother stowing her tapestry wools each in their chintz slot, then rolling these up; my father in his den glancing at his watch and deciding to finish the chapter – and then the procession into the dining-room.

'Time lost' – but still for Agnes time that's her own to take, closer to that of the flowers on the track than to mine.

Time to take out her memories of a lifetime in that house, childhood, hardship, tatting with her mother, the dance after dipping, courtship, marriage, the coffin on the table; to take these out like snapshots one by one, ponder, examine – then paste, as it were, securely in an album.

But also, fittingly, not running away.

She'll bide till they're on with shearing, she says: 'Then Saimon, that's m' nevvy, 's a canny lad as ull not cum hisself. He'll send wi' trailer, I'll pack in back and for a' they'll knaw on roadside it'll be a foreigner passing through.'

Her eyes gleam with the fun of it.

But that's what she'll be where she's going – a 'foreigner'. She'll hate it anywhere else.

She listens, then says 'Get away! That's dale talk is that. Dale thinks a sight too much o' itself. And ye'll knaw reason why? They're frightened is folks in dale. They'll not measure themselves wi' folk outside. They're skeered o' what they dawn't knaw. They'll not taike it on. And I'm not saying there's not sense at back o' it. Ye'll not buy sheep from a strainger as ye'll not knaw what ye'll git. But there's more than sheep in life, there's death ye knaw. And ye'll not knaw much about that when time comes. There's bonny plaices out yonder and best way is fettle yourself wi' what ye dawn't knaw while ye've time to learn.'

9

Yes, I suppose so. In any case I've no option.

All the same with the house like a new pin, and a house-like-a-new-pin-summer stretching ahead and why does the P.E. have to drop his ash wherever he goes and wherever I go a face outside on a ladder looking in (paint and you'll transistor while you work), the P.E. himself whistles off – to the pub in Helwith for cigarettes – while they undercoat his study.

I whistle up to the pike and think about it, watching the clouds pile round a pink lagoon. Cloud-cuckoo-land? Well that's what Agnes thinks. But I've been out yonder, all over. And after a beck in spate what would she make of a concrete lily-pool?

No, *that's* cloud-cuckoo-land.

And language, made by man, does include the word/concept 'sky', *ergo* existence includes a sky. We're 'somewhere under the sky'; and what I am is where – here and now. In place and time. Place, perhaps. But time? Isn't time in fact the antithesis of place – a fluid elastic fabric stretching behind and before, stretching ahead? Perhaps you can tell me why the two were ever run in harness. They aren't. Remove that elastic. Take it away. 'I can't afford the time.' For God's sake don't you see that now is enough is enough is a rose is a rose?

Is the sky.

How can't it matter what's going on up there? When what's happening now won't ever happen again. It's going, going – gone! Don't you see? That if you pin-point, pen-point this it won't be gone for ever? Don't you see how fast you're vanishing? No. Yes. In other ways. Clouds are marginal. There are human, there are more urgent things.

Yes. But all the same, or rather all the more, mightn't an immense feather bed in which you can bounce, sink, submerge – *and* equipped with fountains (and you won't find that in the colour supplements) help? Or a mammoth mushroom whale gliding through your ethos for no reason, no reason at all – wouldn't that help to cut the psychiatrist's bill?

Yes, if you're lucky enough, feather-bedded enough – I'm not.

Well, in that case, feather-headed enough to think you can live on air, well sky. . . . There's no money in clouds. At least you could get down and write *The Day of the Jackal.*

I thought we'd gone into all that. Meanwhile, as I sit here, let me tell you this air is like champagne. And cheaper.

Free?

Well no, everything has its price. But still cheap. And chilled. In fact it's frozen.

Time to go home. The painters must have gone off now. It's dusk already. As I descend from the moor there's the wafer wraith of a new moon; and car-lights in the lane – the man who works in the garage going back to Rigg. But not going back to Rigg, turning into our drive.

He can't be back as late as this.

It's twenty minutes to Helwith. And twenty more to Belgravia in Belldale. You really do live in cloud-cuckoo-land, don't you?

No, no as usual the car's broken down. Meanwhile he's busy with the fire.

'Just take a look at that,' he says proudly, stepping aside to let me see the blaze, 'it was practically out. And you can see how quickly it's come up!'

He goes to fetch in more logs.

'Do you need any help?' I call.

It's too late. he doesn't hear.

Do I need any help?

No, for a mad moment up there I thought I did, but not any more, not here in this room which is ours, with the P.E. bringing in logs, and now, as I draw the curtains – the Room in the Field! I'd forgotten about the Room in the Field and am looking out at this – into the room I know and do not know – when the P.E. staggers in. The log-basket squeaks, moans, subsides, as, putting an arm round my shoulders, he says:

'What on earth are you doing? You can't possibly see a thing out there.'

'Yes I can. Can't you?'

I show him and explain the Room in the Field.

'Well, you see it won't be so bad.'

What won't be? Moving. Moving into what I do not know.

I've already, in fact, moved into this as we sit down and I ask: 'Why were you so late back? Did the car. . . ?' No, it was simply pointless to come home when he couldn't work – so he went and dug the Wrecker's garden.

'It's absurd, of course, when she's being kicked out.'

Kicked out. That's marvellous. 'Why?'

'But I told you. . . .' It's not the sort of news I'd forget.

'Her mother's letting all the cottages on the estate as holiday houses.'

I can't say I like the Honourable Mrs Piers who inhabits the far countree of hunting and racehorses and stately homes and *The Field* and nothing but. Though I suppose it's Safe Land, if, as a debutante, you married a faithless French film director. You might try to jump the park wall but you jumped back pretty quick, nabbed a title and nabbed your hunting hat. Grand though this is in its way, it's not the Wrecker's way: of course she can't write in that cottage; no one could. She can't in Paris either but that's another story, and literally is: a first book before she was twenty which set Paris by the ears, and since then – the glitter of the show.

She ought to get out, they talk too much, they're too articulate.

She ought to sit under an olive tree and rot.

Well that's what her bulging frontal lobes/critical faculties need – a year off under an olive tree.

The P.E. agrees. In that case, why go and dig her garden?

'Because . . .' he says. 'Well, do you know what she's doing? You'll never guess.'

'Redecorating that cottage from top to toe. And sewing, making new curtains. And going to sales.'

He's taken aback; then says 'I'd forgotten I'd told you' (he hasn't). 'But isn't it mad when she knows she's got to leave?'

'Utterly mad.' In my heart of hearts I think it's abnormally normal. But we have, as I've said, much in common, the Wrecker and I.

More than I'd thought, in fact. More now than ever before. More than for years she was faintly prepared to allow. And for two at least after Jason, glittering in Paris, told her she ought to look up the P.E., she did with those huge hollow Holbein-French brown eyes look exclusively at the P.E. I was the wife, meekly at first, then making gaffe after gaffe. Until the time when she came with her current lover. And of course I'd heard of Pierre Blanc. And Pierre Blanc had heard of *me*, had actually read and admired something. So there we were talking our heads off. And though Pierre Blanc didn't last, from then on things were *à trois* and not *à deux*. Since when, it's true, we've had an eyeful of sixes and sevens, thanks to the Wrecker's internal combustion computer. No matter – on to the olive tree and perhaps we can borrow it sometimes. I'll ring and ask her to dinner one night this week.

78

Wednesday. It's pouring. No faces, no transistors. So I seize the day and belt into my study?

Well no, no belting. All the same I do go to my study, end up in this and emerge with the oddest feeling, feeling – of course it's mad – that I've actually found a loophole. Yes, through the paling fence. In fact looping the loop.

My first find was the cheque book. The P.E. had asked for my last one (I suppose, though he didn't say so, the Bank Statement). Anyway I searched and searched, and finally he said mightn't it be the one I'd used in London, in which case couldn't it still be in my London handbag? And it was. Inside Jason's menu.

I sat down with this, or rather with the voluptuous sensation of unfolding a voluminous damask napkin, back laved and bathed afresh in the glamour and glow of that evening, and not just the reprieve from Grandmother's Steps – a sensation that never fails to leap to life with Jason of youth, our common youth; a reprieve in short?

From death? I don't understand. Unless you mean death in life.

Life is where it happens. *That's* Grandmother's Steps.

I'm not on the subject of Death (capital D), you must have snoozed off. I'm talking about a reprieve from the death of a day. Rain. A reprieve, oh from countless things. Which is why, I suppose, idly looking down at Jason's, to me now, arcane 'advice', idly trying to fish up what he'd said Dostoevsky said, I instead land a minnow – a couple I saw that evening in the restaurant and consigned to their proper habitat, oblivion.

They were seated two tables away, aggressively upper-class, the ostrich breed; didn't look at the menu, waved this away (or the man did) and dutifully ate their way through oysters and sole saying – literally nothing. I pointed them out

79

to Jason, who – we were talking about the P.E. – glanced up and dismissed them: 'Holy deadlock.' And they were, of course, by far the most uninteresting people present. So that I can't think why they should haunt me now.

I suppose because they *were* ghosts.

But the woman wasn't quite, despite being so impeccably the part. For an instant I'm positive she was tempted to rebel, recall the waiter and ask to see the menu.

There was also the fact that her 'good clothes' seemed deliberately designed to deny, and did completely obscure, her beauty. Why? She didn't efface herself, on the contrary. She walked out of that restaurant like a queen.

Because she was lost, fearfully lost.

All those people are – underneath.

Yes, but in her it showed.

She was there on sufferance.

How do I know? I don't yet, I'll have to find out.

The point is I actually want to, am in fact rearing to go. For that hole in the paling fence? All right, a bolt-hole. Well mightn't it be one? Note-form, not writing, just working it out. If you've worked it out what's the point of writing it down? The point, my present point is that I'm not writing. Hey diddle diddle . . . old cow, you're miles off the moon!

So what? If I'm up tomorrow by six I can put in two clear hours before the transistors arrive. And see the dawn.

You've left out the cat and the fiddle.

Blast, yes. I'd forgotten: *a three-course meal.* I can't just knock this up, I'm hopelessly out of practice. The P.E. says I'll have to; I don't see why. He says because she always does. I don't see why this means I should fiddle half my day away, fiddle with cookery books, then vichyssoise and goulash. Give her some rope – yes, spaghetti, fruit and cheese.

I'm up at six. *Was she beautiful?* Is she beautiful? Yes, though I didn't notice this until she rose to go and the light caught her hair: *it was Titian red*; but flattened out of existence, smoothed over her ears in a style that was what – late twenties, early thirties?

She's modelled herself on someone – who? Is also in black; in mourning? Or does she always wear black? No, well-cut tweeds. For dinner? Well, it was a suit not a dress. Combine black with hairdo and – I'm getting hot – that makes her in mourning for her mother.

The Mother. The mother will have to wait, though she's obviously important.

But if I don't put out the light I'll miss the dawn.

I sit in the dark and watch it – fire smelting the hills: Hephaistos, the blacksmith, is at his anvil, for Ares is in bed with golden Aphrodite. And wait – yes, here come the chains he has forged 'delicate as cobwebs' to enmesh and trap the lovers in their sleep. A mesh of gold now, for Zeus, the Sun, is watching and has betrayed them, caught and pinioned *in flagrante delicto.* And the gods, well the gods of course stood in the doorway seized by 'unquenchable laughter' at the artifice of cunning Hephaistos.

I don't care what shepherds say, it's the first perfect morning, blue, tranquil. . . .

And I've ruined it. Achieved the almost impossible feat of a row with the P.E., who happened to mention he'd put on the calor gas at five – to warm up the dining-room. You can't warm it up without the central heating, which is why we cook where we sit and eat off our knees; why, in short, the 'For Sale' notice will go up *in eight days.* And I'm damned if I'll have spaghetti sauce smeared all over that table and dropped on those new-pin flags – it soaks in. And after all it's not as if we're having the Queen of Sheba. . . .

If I'd skipped the Queen of Sheba and simply said 'she's an

old friend, she'll understand', he'd have understood. If I'd simply explained, rationally and quietly, about the flags he wouldn't have said 'There's no need to raise your voice'. . . .

The truth is those transistors are getting on both our nerves. If he'd been able to get up and go to his study, there wouldn't have been any row. But on a still day like this you're dogged by the blare wherever they are. And he's gone off to Rigg without our making it up. Grimly, to shop: 'Tomatoes, ham, fruit, cheese, grating cheese (otherwise *small* drum of Parmesan)'.

And now he's back – with grapes! And a huge bunch of flowers! Grapes, for heaven's sake; and flowers, she doesn't need flowers. They aren't. . . . There's a card attached. They're for me.

I go outside and shout 'Could you turn off those transistors? I'm sorry but my husband can't work.'

Lay dining-table. Candelabra. I must say it does look nice. But oh if the cat were away how the mice could play!

We've asked her for seven – an early meal as we can't take late nights, and because this means she'll arrive at a quarter to eight. She does. The P.E. goes out, vanishes out to the car. As usual the jabbering starts, and lasts. In that French little-girl voice. 'There's no need to raise your voice.' My irritation is burning a hole in the curtains when she appears, still talking over her shoulder – crisp white shirt, green sweater, jeans to match, bracelets. The P.E. looming behind her with a basket: wine, olives, pâté, a *hunk* of Parmesan. (Blast that drum of dust.) We embrace warmly:

'Ah, it's so good to see you!' She stands back: 'You look marvellous! And that dress!'

It's darned and twenty years old.

'You mean an original?'

Yes, I was always dressed by Fortuny.

She laughs: 'But seriously, the Chanel look is back. Cécile de Rothschild has bought one exactly like it.'

Seriously, shouldn't I have a place in Madame Tussaud's?

It is my turn now to scan her carefully. She's cut off her hair. It suits her. The effect is somehow blonder. Also more than ever like a *poupée*. But this isn't what I'm looking for: *I think she's all right*. All the same, as a precautionary measure, I'll put some of that pâté out on biscuits.

The P.E. is drawing a cork. They're chattering away. About what? The fire, the chimney doctor.

'You can't leave this house. I so love this house.'

We can't – leave because *she* loves it!

But she's dying to hear my news.

I tell her I've seen Jason.

'Oh that man he is brilliant! And *Liberties*, how do you say, "spot on".'

I don't say it and don't think it, don't say I haven't read it. I say I think he's a badly depressed man.

She looks at me, impressed by the profundity of this remark.

'No, so gay! But you think depressed?' She hasn't read it either. But heard enough about it to suit her book (the one she can't write). This being dangerous ground and her third glass already empty, I say that the spaghetti is *al dente*.

'But this is delicious. What is it?'

A Neopolitan dish – *Spaghetti alla puttanesca*.

I regret it as soon as I've said it, though she doesn't speak Italian and doesn't ask the meaning of *puttanesca*. But the P.E. doesn't need to ask. Insouciance: I gave him a quick glance. It's all right, he's missed it. From now on laissez-faire. In fact I love the story of all those parties, lap up Nathalie (Sarraute) and poor old Marguerite (Duras); literary gossip. What about some ideas? We need them here. She doesn't. They're just what she doesn't need. Well what about some reality – olive trees?

83

The P.E. says what about coffee and going in the other room?

This seems to have been a move in the right direction, the direction of an opening (Never Offer Advice Unless You're Asked) as, making coffee, I hear her say isn't Nelly Moser the best clematis for a north wall.

Now is the time, now is his chance. . . . But all he says is yes. Hold it, just hold on to that clematis:

'Black? Sugar?'

'Please.' She's curled up on the divan, and now lies back on this as if trying it out. Looking round. Musing:

'I don't know what I'd do without you two.'

The P.E. shifts in his leather chair. Well if he won't I will. And my heart does go out to her as she lies, her eyes, like the fizz of her talk at dinner, suddenly stilled, briefly lapped in the happiness of our room.

I move and perch beside her: 'Listen, if you weren't here, you wouldn't need us. It's that wretched cottage.'

'I'll always need you. You're so wise and good.'

More squeaks from leather chair. I press on none the less: 'Well, the advice of the Sybil is drink up your coffee.'

She leans on her elbow and downs this obediently, like Horlicks. It's cold. The P.E. seizes the excuse to beat a retreat and heat some more.

'Have this while it's hot. Now listen. Why don't you get out to Provence?'

Provence is finish; I don't understand: Provence is Paris and worse.

'Well, Tuscany, Umbria, a Greek island. . . .'

But wherever she goes they come – the *beau monde*, the film one, literati, the press, photographers. . . .

I not only think this self-inflating nonsense, I know it is. She doesn't have to tell them where she's gone. Or does she? Yes, of course she does.

And the real, the only explanation of that cottage is an effort to beat herself at her own game.

But it's not a game she can win – there or anywhere else. Because she doesn't *need* to write a book. She wants fame and a man who sticks, and none of them ever does. I can't think why. Actually I can: *vide* Pierre Blanc joking about the exquisite mille-feuille she made and brought to his study – he'd have to move out to work. She wants to be loved but also to outshine the lover, and, when she can't, kills the thing she loves.

I do find it pathetic, but she's piling it on a bit now – this is her infantile ploy/plea for attention. But she's getting none from the P.E. and suddenly, sitting up, swings her legs to the ground:

'I must go.'

Yes, it's midnight. She stands, totters, plops back on divan:

'Do you think I could possibly stay the night?'

In the morning, at least, thank heaven, she's gone – leaving behind no morning; woken by the transistors, leaving a note: 'Forgive me. I just couldn't face going home. Warmest thanks and love. Will ring. . . .'

She wasn't in any condition to go.

But also leaving a trail of debris in her wake. That table! And my spotless flags – it's hopeless. Nothing – Vim, soda, bleach – will get out tomato sauce. It's the oil; it soaks in. I knew it would. And leaving behind three empty bottles, *three* – I'm furious. The P.E., who's moved in on the washing-up, says since she brought one bottle he could hardly refuse when we ran out half-way through the meal. He didn't enjoy the evening any more than I did. Well, I suppose that's something to chalk up.

But not enough; enough, after fighting flags, to fight through a gale. Not enough to blow away the thought that he does enjoy her company – when I'm not there. And he's not enjoying mine this evening either. Although his study's finished, his work hasn't gone well. From six on he's worried she hasn't rung. Then says it's because she's feeling too miserable and guilty; I ought to ring her. I don't see why. Why it won't keep, why she can't be left to stew in her own juice – gin – as she clearly had before she came last night.

He thinks it's my fault about last night.

He says yes, of course she'd drunk too much; but I should have seen this and seen it wasn't the moment to launch in (about the cottage). It was only then that she went so completely to pieces. Then why doesn't he. . . ? Oh very well I'll ring.

I do. How is she? Fine. She's had a marvellous day, has finished (and we must come and see) the curtains, has ordered the Nelly Moser, is laughing, spirited. The P.E. takes the receiver from me, and in a moment he, too, is laughing, spirited, quoting Braudel, sharing some learned joke.

I don't see the joke.

And haven't – not that she's asked – had a marvellous day.

No, it's the P.E. now who doesn't see – that she hasn't asked, hasn't thanked; has got back on the gin and doesn't remember a thing about the evening.

When he rings off at last and I say this, he says no, she has to forget. A highly convenient doctrine if you share it.

I don't share it. And don't intend to have her for two evenings running.

Where am I going? To fetch the ironing-board.

10

4 a.m. I don't want to see the dawn, what I want is not to. A wretched night and ahead a wasted day. Write both off. Write? I couldn't possibly. Two hours sleep simply isn't enough.

If you get down something the night/day won't have been entirely wasted.

Well try some black coffee. I'm trying it, treacle black.

The day yawns, glimmers between the drawn curtains. I've no desire to look out, still less look in. So where can I look? At the Mother. She's neither in nor out. I can't remember where the heck she was.

There wasn't one in that restaurant. Are you certain? Positive. Flip back. There was one there, like Banquo's ghost.

The Mother: on whom she's modelled herself.

Or been dominated by?

Which? Both?

Obviously forceful. Arch snob. Plays Bridge. Plays the invalid.

And, when alone, plays Patience in the dark. Why? Because that's what I'm doing myself. She must have been able to see. Yes, small pink lamp drooping its light on the cards.

Meaning she holds the cards? You don't when you're playing Patience. The pack's face down.

She does hold the cards.

It's too dark to make out the rest of the room. Wait till your eyes adjust. Yes, it's coming clearer now: a jungle – of tub-chairs, small tables (stools?) hexagonal (?), elaborately carved. *The gleam of a Benares brass tray.*

She can't – habit acquired in India – stand the light. India. Yes that would explain the Bridge.

And explain her contempt for men. The Fifth Gurkhas are different, a cut above. But unfaithful all the same. Her father, then her husband. All those 'upright Englishmen'. . . .

So that's why she opposed the daughter's marriage. To Edward (?), made of wood, military moustache – wood chippings – chip off the old block. There's no other explanation of why else she opposed this so strongly. He wasn't a lord? But was patently suitable.

All the same she did oppose – and so *ensure* – the marriage.

Because Frances, daughter, *had* hated Mother. Then, when marriage failed, swung around. Yes. Well isn't that it?

So we won't, after all, hang together, the Wrecker and I.

And tonight there's no trace of debris. The painters left at midday, since when the P.E. has got on swimmingly, has written and read me five pages – and only then reveals that these are the start of his final chapter! Of course I'm thrilled. At this rate he thinks he could be through, out of *The Sack* inside three weeks.

I'm sorely tempted to risk it, but after the last two evenings can't afford to risk the perfection of this one. And, in fact, swiftly shed any desire to do so, do anything more than sit in our shadow-land, watching his face, watching the fire, hearing its still small voice: 'Wait, now isn't the time'; no, I'm learning.

I've only three weeks to wait and then we'll be able to talk. Because it is – well isn't it grotesque that we've no plan, no notion of where we'll go? Whenever I've raised, tried to raise the subject he's side-stepped this: 'We can't' – and we can't, of course – 'afford a mortgage.' He can, does, has to forget, has put his head in *The Sack* and won't so much as discuss where we'd like to live. I'm off the Cambridge semi after Wimbledon. 'The value of travel is fear'. Camus says. Yes, that disorientation which restores a Here and Now. But we aren't travelling anywhere; and can't afford to store the furniture either.

I look round our room and think you couldn't store this anyway. Sudden uprush of unreality. With eight days to go before we're 'For Sale' I, too, don't believe it will happen.

Death did come for the Archbishop.

Meanwhile? Meanwhile I walk looking my last on all things lovely – sheep, walls, clouds marbling the hills? Yes, but these are no longer events. It's as if the lines were down. Seeing as you do from a car, as a stranger sees.

Only an imperative need to get out of the house drives me, drags me today as far as the beck, to revisit the larches, my ancient mermaids with their shagreen trunks peering through their still grey matted hair.

I suppose the spring always is more like an autumn here, because in autumn the leaves, ripped off by the gales, fall while they're still green. And now as I look round the dale green trees mingle with ghost trees, cobweb trees, in their way beautiful. . . .

But chiefly I'm confined to preserving pins as new, or, housebound by house-agents ringing, to the bolt-hole; and whichever, whatever I'm doing interrupted by the Wrecker's daily, twice daily telephone calls.

I say he can't, he says he won't until he's out of *The Sack*. All right I'll go and see those make-believe curtains. He says we'll go, but just for a drink. That's the last thing I want to go for. She says she's only ringing for a chat. She's reading Malcolm Lowry. Have I read Malcolm Lowry? No, I've tried and tried.

'But it's all about us.'

89

Us. I don't care for the concept. Since when has she learnt to use it? No she means, always means all about her. All about drink, drinking and not being able to write. We have nothing in common, the Wrecker and I.

6 a.m. *Why did marriage go wrong?* Because it couldn't go right. Bond: both were hopelessly tied up. Married for tennis, not love. Also, in her case, because her friends all had, because one did.

But a lot of those marriages do get through. Why didn't this one?

Tweeds. She'd lived in the country [Where? Reserve.]. Hated London (small flat). Restless. Nothing to do. Frigid. Bored stiff. Shy, hated parties. Missed riding. *Missed slopping about in old mac and gumboots.* Picture beginning to take shape.

Freckles – embarrassed by these, which confirm her belief in murmurs: 'Hard to believe she's her mother's daughter. . . . Astonishingly plain, apart from the hair, of course, and she doesn't even take any trouble with that. . . . So disappointing for Adèle (?). And yes, *isn't* it odd when Adèle is quite the most elegant woman one knows. . . . If any girl needed a finishing-school. . . . They couldn't supply the cheek-bones. No, but it's marvellous what six months in Vevey will do. . . .'

She's unfinished – still in the raw; gauche, innocent. In other words she will be vulnerable, easy prey.

Enter Lover.

Of course that's it – why she was there on sufferance.

Dash it! The 'phone's been ringing for hours.

I have to answer this in case it's the house-agent. It is. We still have two days left to go. But Egglestone has a client who's leaving for London tomorrow. Would this afternoon be possible? Yes, I'm bound to say yes; bound to clear up my study and to turf the P.E. out of his. Since he's never out of it and can't bear his papers disturbed I never get in and the dust is never disturbed. He says it can't be disturbed now. Well, he'll do it himself. Later. He can't; he won't even see the stains on the carpet. Looking exhausted, distracted, he says when are these people coming? At two. In that case he'll take himself off to the pub.

I say he can't. I can't – show people over the place for the first time alone; he ought to be here. A man inspires confidence where a woman doesn't. I can't explain anything legal.

I'm upset, plead, wax hot then cold.

So of course he goes.

Of course he can't take interruptions at this stage. He's holding too many threads in his mind. At least he can think in the pub.

No, he's even more upset than I am.

And now I'm upset that we've quarrelled – twice within a week.

Am also, after an hour in that study, filthy. Quick, I'll have to change. Do something about my hair. Hairpins everywhere. My hand's shaking.

And now they're here. Rich, discreet (grey) Rolls rolls down drive. Rush downstairs, totter to the door.

There's a man outside. Look round. No, there's only the man. Tall, distinguished looking.

'Do come in.'

He does, bent almost double. Operation Jack-knife. Unfortunate start. Pinion him in porch and point our date over inner door – 1685.

'This would have been the original front door?'

Yes, contemporary. . . . We brought it inside to preserve it.

He nods, admiring the great wide gale-faring timbers. Says it's like wood you pick up by the sea. Not a line to pursue.

91

'And this' – this is my trump card – 'is the bolt.' I pull it out from the wall, an immense wooden crow-bar.

'Good heavens! You're certainly safe.' Safe as houses?

I purl away about the Scots invading from the north as he follows me into the drawing-room we've ceased to use.

'What a superb room. . . ! And what a view!'

He's starting across to the window, then turns and holds out his hand:

'My name is', one I couldn't get over the 'phone, 'Vivers, Philip Vivers.'

Odd name, too odd to forget. I've heard it before somewhere. Can't think where.

'It's immensely good of you to let me come today. But I've admired your house for years.'

Admired it shooting over the moor. Bony ascetic face.

'I'll lead the way.' Start to, up the stairs. No back: 'I'm so sorry, I've forgotten the dining-room.' And the kitchen (a room we don't use either).

'This is the kitchen. . . .'

'"Cum breakfast-room".' He's holding, consulting the brochure; is smiling:

'Would you like me to take you round?'

Abruptly wake up to the fact that he's extraordinarily goodlooking. Rather chilled by this than otherwise. If he thinks he can trade. . . . We're both in trade, and trade let it be:

'It's just that we don't have breakfast in here ourselves.'

A shade feeble, but coolly.

Up to the P.E.'s study: 'This must have been one of the doorways you raised?'

'Yes.'

How on earth does he know about the doors? I certainly never told Egglestone since, with the house scheduled, structural alterations were strictly *verboten*.

'And now we're in the byres?'

92

'Yes, we converted these. . . .' He does seem to know the house almost better than I do.

We're round to my red and white quilts: 'As you see it's open-plan, self-contained; we did it for our children. Also for visitors. They can get up when they want, stay as long as they want, get their own breakfast. . . .'

We don't have visitors. I can't stay as long as I want. I suddenly desperately want a cigarette.

Back at last to the drawing-room.

'I forgot the linen-cupboard. But perhaps you'd like to poke round on your own. It's in the first bathroom.'

'I'll take your word for it.'

In other words he isn't interested – or only in the view; is still standing, musing, looking out, absently fishing in breast-pocket, fishing out cigarette-case, extracting, starting to tap one on this:

'Forgive me. Do you mind if I smoke?'

'I was just going to have one myself.'

'Can I offer you one of these? I'm afraid they're Gitanes.'

A Gitane!

'Do sit down.'

'I can't use Virginia tobacco.' Leans forward to give me a light, no easy task. My hand still thinks it's an aspen leaf.

'I'm sorry, but it's the first time I've had to do this.'

'And you don't, of course, want to sell? I'm not surprised. But if you do, I'll buy it.' Flat – no talk of surveys.

I'm suddenly rowing hard against the tide: 'But you've shot here in the summer. I don't think you realize. In the winter you can be snowed in for days.'

'Snowed in. Let me see. . . .' Crosses his legs, amused, flicks through brochure: 'You'll have to put it in: "Owners guaranteed to be snowed in for days." Meanwhile your cigarette's out. Let me give you another.'

It isn't a cigarette. He's exercising his very considerable

93

charm. *He wants me to want him to have the house*. Well, two can play at that game. Keep rowing. Reset compass. Veer north. Lean back, crossing my legs:

'So you've lived a lot in France?'

'Well, no, I've never actually lived in France. Though at one time, as a boy, I hoped I was going to.'

'So it's pure romanticism, your smoking Caporal? As is your thinking you'd like to buy this house.'

'No, it's an odd story. I won't bore you with it.'

He doesn't bore me.

It's an extraordinary story.

In fact I can't wait to get into my study and write it down.

You've already got a story on your hands.

Yes, but this ties in with it, ties in perfectly.

'So now I know why you smoke Gitanes!'

It works. He's getting up: 'Forgive my staying so long. But will you, at least, give me first option? I'll pay the full price. Your agents have my address. But I'll leave you my card all the same.'

11

He'll give us the full price! If only the P.E. . . . . But he won't risk returning for half an hour at least.

It's too quick. Things can't happen like that. It's as if a guillotine had fallen between today and yesterday.

Go upstairs and write down that story while it's still fresh in your mind. I go upstairs, and try. And can't, of course; can't now think why I wanted to write it down.

> . . . That was in another country
> And besides the wench is dead.

No, what I want is to expunge.

But things do happen like that. Not this one; I won't let it. You, sir, think this a house like any other, a static affair plumped down like a sofa on a lawn. You think it's a shelter from the blast? A place to sleep? My dear chap, you won't get a night's sleep here (or not if I have any say in the matter). You'll wheel with the stars, with the wheeling hills, reel as the earth reels, tossed like a dog in a blanket; and sick as a dog. 'Rolled round . . . with rocks and stones and trees' – it's hardly your form I think, much as I should relish the spectacle.

Lord, he was cool. Yes, a cool customer. Well, as I've said, two can play at that game. Just because he wants it commits me to nothing at all.

I didn't say I'd give him first option.

And shan't disturb the P.E. by saying he asked for it, more than that 'they' came. . . . I'll cook up something.

Perversely this is made easier by the fact that he himself won't, I know, be interested till the evening. And isn't. Assuming I'm out, he's gone straight to his study.

Put my nose round the door of this, but only because he'd wish it, is always uneasy in an empty house and will be doubly so today in a haunted one. This is why the P.E. keeps me on course. Because if you've fought a war in the jungle it's a thing you find hard to do, and, knowing this, you evolve ways and means. Which is different from not knowing, which wouldn't keep me on course – which which-wise isn't the tongue Fielding wagged. Nor the one the P.E. is trying to wag, desperately hanging on to, i.e. trying to hang on to, *The Sack of Rome*, or even his last sentence, as, looking up, he asks:

'How did it go? What were they like?'

'All right. . . . Impossible.'

'You must tell me all about it later.'

I shan't, of course. Meanwhile I think I will go out. Instead downstairs stand rooted by the window: immense black clouds like a bush-fire against a silver sky. It's the first thing I've really *seen* for weeks.

But a fake bush-fire all the same. Why do you need a house? Why not simply buy a box at the opera, or bed down in any theatre (cloak-rooms, refreshment bar)? Well that's what Hemingway's Brett whoever she was in real life which I can't remember did in the *Vieux Colombiers*. Why don't you actually try some reality?

I'm trying it now as I turn and see the books on the table. Two. Lying there quite openly. Openly Malcolm Lowry: *Under the Volcano* and *Hear Us O Lord from Heaven Thy Dwelling Place*.

A sharp but distinct earthquake. I'd forgotten the Belldale Vesuvius, now briefly erupting, disrupting:

He did say the pub.

But also brought you those books back.

Also I'm bound to give the Wrecker her due. The titles, at least, ironically are as she puts it 'all about us', however volcanic her part in making this so.

I pick up *Hear Us O Lord*, both for obvious reasons and because this is a Lowry new to me. Apparently short stories. *Through the Panama*. That's what I'm going through too. And actually is:

> Games of chess now seem to me utterly unreal and something like that eerie wonderful absurd scene in. . . . *The Fall of the House of Usher* in which Roderick Usher and the old doctor are reading by the fire, the house has already caught fire, not only that but cracks are opening in the walls and the house is in fact coming to pieces all around them, while flames creep . . . along the carpet, an insane electric storm, moreover, is discharging its lightnings outside in the swamp, through which Mrs Usher . . . , having just risen from the grave, is making her way back to the house. . . .

Our clients are cooked to a turn, crackling like Charles Lamb's pork, as, dimly aware of movements overhead, I glance up – and realize that I haven't for three hours, haven't so much as once glanced out of the window. When did I last read a book, so lose myself in one that I forget to draw the curtains? It's black glass night outside, and the P.E. who now draws these. All the same, isn't he down early?

Yes, because he wants to hear. . . . I'm wrong. He turns on the wireless and listens all the way through the shipping forecast (East-North-East, Dreadnought in the Pennines – Gale Force Nine) all through the weather (Ireland, Isle of Wight), Big Ben at last but still askew (and the RSPCA really should have got those chimes right now), all through

Whitelaw, *all through Whitelaw*, on to Mick McGahey – all through the Stocks and Shares we don't possess. And he doesn't even notice the glass I've put beside him.

'Have some whisky.'

He doesn't. Instead he says:

'I suppose you didn't tidy away any papers this morning?'

Papers? In his study when I cleaned this.

No, his study isn't like mine. There's no need to tidy. I simply lifted, dusted and put things back.

'You're certain you didn't move anything round?'

Absolutely certain.

He can't find some vital references.

'Have you looked in the linen-cupboard, tried the clothes-peg basket?'

Smiles: 'Yes, of course they're bound to turn up. All the same, if you don't mind, I think I'll go back upstairs.'

We both go. Aren't they perhaps inside a book, the cover of one he's using? There are thirty; we look through these.

Cheerfully he says 'Don't worry. I'll find them tomorrow.'

Let's eat and go early to bed. Roast clients? By now they're cremated. The afternoon is as if it had never been.

An omelette. The sweets of oblivion. Woman, what more do you want?

Nothing. His being less *distrait*. Less remote.

'How was Suzette?'

He's no idea. Wasn't there a letter? He hasn't. . . . She'd left the books for him at the pub.

Out – out to my gilded hills, gilded as never before. Give and it shall be given unto you. And oddly is. Dispossessed I'm once more in possession of a land I'd begun to think I'd invented or dreamed.

Why is it accurate to describe the sky as steep here? But it is;

this morning a steep gun-metal grey, the metal going rusty in places, cloud-wrack rusted by sunrise. And then the whole of the skyline a line of beacons, clouds on fire now flashing the news that day has beaten night and bringing the Andes captive in its train. Mexico's back, steep, stony, russet, Prussian blue. It's as if I'd been blind and now had eyes to see.

He thinks he can buy this up.

No, he's made you a gift of the place.

It's he who's given you back the power to see.

Also bequeathed you that story. Go home and write it down. Well why not? Why not if it suits your book? And it does suit your book.

To transpose or not transpose?

No, first of all straight – as he gave it:

1939. Outbreak of war. Father immediately volunteered; tragically (scrap 'tragically') killed Anzio '44. Meanwhile 1940–43, Free-French officer billeted on Mother, though often away for weeks on mysterious missions. Hero-worshipped by son (client) then aged five-seven. Frenchman establishes close rapport with child (apple of Mother's eye), but Mother seemingly always in a hurry – is also intensely English, reserved, shy; no time to give to Frenchman. Fends him off, i.e. is violently attracted. Then, at end of three years, succumbs – goes Free French with a vengeance of one erotic week (predictably week before D-Day). They don't expect ever to meet again.

But child has hero's home address and, after end of war and Father's death, writes to him in France. Corresponds. Visit from Frenchman. Love affair resumed and marriage arranged. Wedding to take place quietly in England, but will live in France. All packed. Trunks in hall. Week before wedding bridegroom and his father both killed in car-crash (telegram from French Intelligence).

Six years later boy (client), by then aged fifteen, sent out to French family to learn language. And ran into his hero in the street. But didn't believe latter dishonourable: thought his hand had been forced, that he knew and was known to have told mother too much. Client continued to visit him for years.

Still, as he told it, seems to me weak. In need of an explanation – which I have: the love affair was with Frances, forwarded, procured by Mother both as revenge on 'upright Englishmen'; also vicariously. She, too, was in love with Frenchman. But then when it came to Frances (divorced by Edward) marrying Pierre (?), Mother's jealousy got the better of her. *It was she who laid on that telegram*. How? I don't know yet. Wait for tomorrow morning's next thrilling instalment, 6 a.m.

All my new-found ebullience goes up in smoke, alias the smell of soup, which meets me outside my study door.

At ten to one. But he's never down before five past. Besides. . . .

Those references. They'd gone clean out of my head. And I don't need his face to tell me that these have failed to turn up. I'm stricken; and not only stricken but doubly so. Since the implication is obvious: they were there yesterday morning before I cleaned his study, and aren't now.

I swear, and again wish I hadn't, that I moved nothing. He doesn't actually say 'don't raise your voice'. All the same I can tell that this did, on the word 'nothing', rise, and jar on the P.E.'s nerves like the screech of brakes. But I didn't. . . . Tears of self-pity are wobbling behind my eyes. Stop that:

'Why not ring the London Library? Now. No, I know they won't over the 'phone. But they've done it before if it's urgent. . . .'

It's useless. He can't remember the sources.

100

He'll have to go to London and hunt for these himself, and if necessary go on to Cambridge. It's my fault, well it must be:

'You mean you'll go tomorrow?'

He won't commit himself; I can't think why. He's stuck till he gets those references.

Yes, but going tomorrow means setting the alarm at 5 a.m. to allow for the hazards of cows meandering to be milked, sheep, hay unloading, British Rail. And, frustration apart, he's dog-tired. You've only to look at him. I do look – sick at heart, sick at heart.

The bloom's gone from the day. Restless, it's pointless to walk. Pointless. What do I mean by pointlessness? With the P.E. back upstairs I sink down in the window, abstractedly aware of birds on the wall emerging from, vanishing back into its lime-green lichened crannies. I suppose tits. I suppose nesting.

Less watching than not watching, I'm suddenly shocked into seeing – seeing stone turn to feathers, flutter and fluff. This must be what visions are like, angels, revelations – as now arriving when you least expect them. To expect a revelation is a contradiction in terms.

And it's not just the transfiguration, the coming alive, quickening of that stone. It's all the small to-ing and fro-ing of birds, instinct with pointlessness. The joy of it! *The point is pointlessness.*

Don't you see – all the dull routine things, the worst, the fearful things, the weapons of war devised in laboratories, are all of them things with a point, a deadly point?

To sing like a bird – why not?

To circle, gliding like gulls, the curlew, apparently purposelessly.

That all one's writing should be as seemingly purposeless as birdsong.

If not, won't one have no 'bird life' left?

101

He's gone at last and I'm thankful, and upset that I am – thankful to have him out of the house. I can bear with his absence but never with his remoteness; inspired though this was, as I knew, guessed, not by any resentment, simply by his own depleted state, a state which made him incapable of decisions, of relating to anything – me or his own dilemma. 'For each foot it's own shoe' is a lesson he long ago learnt, and for most of the past two days I suspect he snoozed.

Nonetheless with the sense of his study as, if not locked against me, in the last resort impenetrable, weighing like a dead lead bell, a dead weight in the house, it was fruitless to go into my own.

For two days I've simply hung on, hanging on to the bell-ropes. But now I'm free. So why should I be upset? He'll come back with the references and meanwhile I'm alone, which is different from being with your loved one and alone.

Alone and free. Well, why shouldn't I – take a day off myself, dare to take hold of the sensation? Won't it strengthen? Won't I have more to offer when he comes home? Why shouldn't I leave the agent to marry or burn?

It's windless, a grey silk morning, the larches tilting their pagodas, aslant, askew. A day of silhouettes – byres, the rise of the moor. . . . Below, perhaps only because one knows these are there, toy houses, the Methodist chapel like its own ghost, dreamt, intangible, frail among the trees.

As if the dale had drawn a thread of grey silk through its needle defining, but barely defining, earth and sky.

In other words a perfect day to climb to the summit of Karva, an assault I seldom have the time to make; and sit there thinking Karva thoughts, partaking of Karva's dreams, as foreign as those of Africa or Spain.

But first must come the descent. I embark on this obliquely

through fields still wan and yellow after the snow, but in which I'm no longer harassed and hustled by haggard hungry sheep as I would have been six weeks ago. Fat lambs grown bold run races, their mothers, fed on pellets, doing no more than glance up as I pass. Despite this it's like being in church: the whole dale resounds with bleating, an endless bell-like complaint – about what?

I'm nearing the head of the old stone track, and preparing to turn down this, when suddenly it dawns on me – they're shearing. In that case Agnes. . . . She's given me no address.

But I don't want to say good-bye, don't want to see her go, don't want to pass that house.

Or climb Karva.

There's no point any longer. I wanted Karva thoughts, wanted to go alone without myself; without, above all, the thoughts, verging on panic, which now seize me – that soon I, too, like Agnes will be gone.

I need to talk to someone and the person I need is the Wrecker. And not just because there's no one else. Isn't it that? Well yes, in a way; dales folk don't up sticks, tear themselves up by the roots – or read Lowry. Doesn't Lowry himself, it occurs to me, say something relevant here; something about seeing other people as shadows, oneself as the only reality; and say that these shadows are often menacing?

Of course; shadows are. It's I who've invented the Wrecker, I who've denied Suzette her reality, her daylight substance, and cast her as a threatening shade when she's merely a woman in distress. As I am; or was. For already as I pad, still in my gumboot socks, to the telephone, I'm calmer for no good reason. I'm still moving house. Yes, but I've turned one shadow into substance.

Shadows into substances. She must be in the garden. Why don't I simply go, drive across? No, she could be out shopping. I'll wait and ring again. Anyway she's sure to ring me.

103

Shadows into substances. But it doesn't always help. I don't want the substance of leaving here. I'd rather have the shadow. What else does Lowry say? (Where did I put. . . ? I didn't. It's under the bed.)

Something about a mountain lion of which he wasn't afraid because he was more afraid of something else. No, no that's not the passage. All the same, of what was he 'more afraid'?

Read on, read back, but remain unclear. Must discuss this with Suzette. She's bound to be in soon. Meanwhile return to Lowry and think he was 'more afraid' of what he calls 'the horrendous self-observation', the honesty creative work demands; of the agonizing effort, one which both 'drove' and 'killed' him – 'to die through it that I might become reborn'.

Yes, yes that's it, mountain lions apart – why one does it, tries to do it at all.

Why he drank. Why Suzette. . . . Dial her, book in hand, my eye sliding to the opposite page:

'Ortega has it that a man's life is like a fiction that he makes up as he goes along.'

In that case shouldn't fiction itself reflect this fiction? And if so (she's still not answering. Odd); if you include, admit this fact into your fiction won't much of the effort fall away? Because you'll be dispensing with a premise that's false from the start.

I'm back to my birds and 'bird life'. To my novel? What of the plot, false premise, false trails, I'm so busy spawning up there? How do I equate these machinations with birdsong? Hadn't I better go upstairs and find out?

There's no need to go upstairs. No, why not light the fire? I can think just as well down here.

You can't, without a pen in your hand.

Yes, I'll still need a pen. In fact what I need at this moment is something to eat.

But first a fire. Fire, will you go for me, too, or deal me out smuts? Firelighter, sticks from the beck, two nice charred logs – and it's taken the bait, it's ablaze! Pile on a huge new log. Sit back and savour the beauty of my fire; of lighting fires because one wants to not because one must? Why can't I make everything like this? Ironing, scrubbing flags? I'm too idle, glowing, happy, hungry to pursue the point.

'Tell me, where is Fancy bred'? Soup? No, I'm fancy-free. Free to fancy olives, mortadella washed down by a glass of Muscadet? Well no, not quite; but free for toasted cheese. Free to lick my fingers. Delicious. This is heaven. And poor old Suzette having lunch with the Honourable. Well she has to sometimes, and obviously she must be. Come, come, woman, this will never do. Wash up your plate – no leave it. Well at least wash your fingers, pick up your pen and make an effort to think.

All right, but don't hustle me. Wait. What is Ortega actually saying? One can't just gobble that down like toasted cheese. It's a strange, a very strange statement. Is my life 'like a fiction'? Do I make it up as I go along? Remake, yes, but not make; and can only remake by writing in order, as Lowry says, 'to be born anew'. But 'makes up as he goes along' – does this refer to choice? Choice is in short supply and always conditioned – by what we are, are born and do not choose to be.

All the same. . . . Yes? Isn't my life like a fiction, one which I make up as I go along, make out of what the day brings; and doesn't the man in the office do the same?

I'm on to something. I've got it. 'Man's life is like a fiction that he makes up as he goes along', i.e. it resembles a fiction in that his beliefs, hopes, desires change as he goes through life according to his age, as if he made these up. Well, it's true, of course. But I don't see that this helps.

A false trail. I was banking on a sense of fiction.

Wouldn't this take you further from birds and birdsong?

105

Trollope lets his characters make it up as they go, scavenging for husbands and position; with no sense of this as a fiction. Their illusions, fantasies, are as solid as the breakfasts they consume. Socially they're secure. Mine are insecure.

Isn't that what you want? Yes and no.

Trollope's are more like the birds in my wall; and he sang it like a bird. Sat in the train and purled away like a thrush.

I couldn't sit or sing anywhere but here.

And suddenly can't sit here. It's four o'clock.

Surely Suzette must be back by now.

But she still isn't answering; and hasn't rung me.

Her 'phone's out of order. Of course that's it. Ring Faults.

It isn't.

She's gone to London with the P.E.

12

It's like being knifed – the shock of his duplicity.

The discovery that he, of all people (no, like anyone else), should be capable of it.

He whom I in great part loved for the reason that he wasn't – capable of so much as a white lie.

I thought he was utterly guileless, gullible to a fault, and that this was why he didn't see – that the Wrecker can't stand other people being happy or creative, that from the start she was bent on breaking us up.

Palpably for the first three years. And then when I went away (blithely, to take out Giles and Mark from school) and she carnally nearly succeeded, he told me so.

I thought we'd put this behind us then. Marriage isn't a bar to enjoying the company of the other sex. He didn't conceal his enjoyment of hers, and, not being my husband's keeper, I made no attempt to sever the Belldale connection.

On the contrary, I sought on my side to cultivate this, took myself to ringing her for a chat, driving across to see her alone. Making my foe my friend? Yes, I thought one of my closest friends.

It wasn't difficult. She wasn't drinking then, could afford to sit back and wasn't, with youth on her side, agonized by the need to repeat her early success, but tranquilly building the nest in which she would do so. Enjoying the nesting I don't enjoy, tranquilly pondering, waiting (as I admiringly thought) until she was ready.

I was wrong of course. Writing is a writer's Swedish Drill.

She'd already pondered too long, too elaborately. . . .

Wrong as on other counts. Cloud-cuckoo-land? Of course there's a cuckoo in the nest.

To think how neatly he covered his tracks. . . .

'Digging her garden' he called it. I'm going to be sick – and am, in the sink.

Rinse out my mouth and perch, shivering, by the fire.

Why should the P.E. be different from other men? Why should I be immune from the fate of all ageing wives? Why do I think of him as the P.E.? Because I've made exorbitant demands on his love and patience. I've asked for this; of course he needs a break. A break? No, a let-up. You're going to accept this, learn from it – and do the thing in style.

Yes. . . .

I could ring Charlotte. . . .

Well he did, reluctantly (Wimbledon being where and what it is) arrange in my hearing to stay there, and lay on Giles for the evening.

Cambridge could be a blind for staying at the Ritz.

Yes. Dial Charlotte. . . . Everyone can't be out. Don't the boys swim on Tuesdays after school? This isn't very stylish. No, but practical. Be practical and have a cup of tea. I do. It's not cheap time yet. What excuse could I give Charlotte? No, I'll have to wait till after six.

An hour and a half to go. How do I fill that in? By reading. I couldn't possibly – when, for all I know, he's in the Ritz now. He can't be; that's where Jason goes. Jason wouldn't care. I shouldn't care. Anyway he's in the London Library. Where he met me. And now has a date with the Wrecker. . . .

Stop wincing. But wherever I look is pain.

In that case stop looking. Put your head in a book with a plot that really grips.

The Aspern Papers?

No, stronger meat.

But I don't, I can't read thrillers.

Of course not, it's all more tenuous. Virginia Woolf, Proust. . . .

They aren't tenuous.

Well, go upstairs and look on Mark's shelves.

Green Penguin: *The Big Sleep*. You've never read Raymond Chandler? My child, you've certainly got a lot to learn – such as the fact that I *am* gripped, so gripped I forget the time. It's brilliant!

And the P.E. who rings me.

Well, he sounds like the P.E. How am I? How's the fire? Am I warm? He's fine, has got the books. And they're all three dining with Jason. No, he won't need to go on to Cambridge. Could I meet him tomorrow at 3.15?

I don't walk, I float from the phone. . . . Lord, Lord I'm happy!

So happy I think I'll have a glass of wine, if there is any. What, drink alone? I won't be, that's just the point. And isn't it one that calls for a celebration?

Possibly the wine was a mistake; or wasn't. At all events, back on the divan, and – happily back to our room – unable to resist going back to Chandler, I can't think why it suddenly dawned on me. Perhaps, as I read, the words of Chandler's title, 'The Big Sleep', unconsciously dimly penetrated.

But it did simply suddenly dawn – with shame, what a fool I'd been; with remorse, how unfair to the P.E. And, in the process ruined the day for no reason at all.

Why do I get everything out of proportion?

Because I exist in a vacuum where my feelings have full sway, sit on a see-saw. This has got to stop. How? By leading a 'normal life'? I can't. Writers don't. If they did they'd get no writing done.

You don't get much writing done.

No, I tick over slowly.

109

Doesn't your adrenalin need a boost?

If you mean Kentish Town and cocktail parties, no.

But seeing Hermione and Nell occasionally?

Perhaps. But not Kentish Town. There are bonnier places out yonder. Not within reach of Hermione and Sybil and Nell.

And not within reach of my purse if you're thinking of Suffolk or Sussex. Besides that wasn't what Agnes was actually saying. She was saying you have to have courage, and you need it to take what comes. But baulking and brooding is a waste of time. Wasted because you've soiled, despoiled, soured the Falernian wine of a Here and Now that will never come again.

So it's come home to roost with a vengeance, my very *raison d'être*. I can't afford these undisciplined squads of emotion. As a wife, as a writer. . . .

And the cure, I suppose, is Chandler's. A clean plot with clean lines, and no strings attached. Inner strings.

But those strings exist in everyone. Yes, but we don't see them. What we see is an external world.

I don't. I guess all the time at what goes on in people. But it's still only guesswork, reading in. Reading yourself into others. Into Jacob? Into Judith? Even the dale presents an elaborate façade.

People are capable of things you would never guess.

Yes, yes we've heard that one before. And know it to be true.

Well, return to the birds on your wall: nothing betrays their tryst with foreign lands. You may see them mysteriously flocking, planning their flight formation – and encounter your swallow in Africa. But don't you see the difference, that in this way you see *more*, more truthfully?

Perhaps. Yes, I think I'm starting to see.

Face it, that as physical beings we are separate, secret, other; that every writer must do as Chandler does – observe and let

110

the externals leak the information which people though they kiss will never tell.

Narrative, in short: spare, factual, fast-moving. I can't; it's not my *métier*. *Métier?*

Well, *toujours la politesse*. I somehow thought we were talking about your disastrous limitations.

Listen, the medicine is under your hand, upstairs in your study. Take it, starting tomorrow at 6 a.m.

13

Wake at eight; and only then woken by the light, sunlight flaring through my curtains!

Outside the whole field littered by what might be cuttlefish – in fact whitened and fattened by fat white gulls, feeding but also gliding through the champagne morning.

I can't possibly waste this in my study.

You'll have to. But first a nip at least of that champagne – and encounter with a caterpillar, emerald with gold spots in pairs, gaudy as a snake, sliding, heaving itself forward in that conveyer-belt way which would be so terrifying if it were large and not small.

'The man of action starts from a sense of paralysis' (Malraux). Quotation from a copy of Mark's thesis, come at last today by the post while I was out! Can't possibly resist a nip of this. Though why doesn't Malraux come clean and say 'the man of violence', since the action he has in mind is murder, inspired by his own predicament, need – not by a sense of judgement? Isn't Malraux in fact describing hysteria? 'The hysterical woman starts from a sense of paralysis.' Why – and consider its verbal derivation – should violence only in women by hysterical? What does Malraux think he is talking about?

What, more to the point, does my son think he's talking about (thankful though I am to be let off Kepler)? 'Trapped within an indifferent world, estranged from his fellow men, [man] is trapped within the prison of self'.

Hum. A shade too near the bone. Besides, I must read not dip. Besides. . . . Well, of course, I'm prevaricating. Why? I

112

suppose it's the shadow of the Cool Customer. But he, at least, *is* a shadow and not substance, substantial though he thinks himself. You lapped it up at the time. And your business is metamorphosis.

Yes. 1939. Is Edward in the army (*vide* moustache)? No, barrister. But as keen Territorial swiftly commissioned and safely disposed of – where? I've got it: posted to Legal Section in India.

Frances lets London flat and thankfully escapes home – to mac, gumboots, horses, celibacy; less thankfully to housekeep, wait hand and foot on Mother (still playing Bridge and Patience in the dark, and still, if 'crippled', at forty-six immaculate – *Bette Davis*.)

N.B. Home – *place*? Establish where. 'Couden' (?), near Bexhill. 'Box' or do I mean 'Bex'? No definitely 'Bex': unfashionable, cheap. Couden cheapest, three miles sea. Pocket India, traditional resort for holidays, retirement. Mother president of Club (malicious delight in dangling, withholding, confining membership to the elect).

Wartime; large house left servantless. Cooking, rationing, war-work. F. also teaching son, aged five, to ride. But happiest moments alone and free in the evening haying horses. Hair invariably soaked by rain or mist. Free not to bother or care. Then, July 1940, Free-French officer billeted on them. Considered a 'catch' by girls who work with Frances in canteen and tease her – don't believe it when she says she wouldn't know him in the street. In fact barely does so in the house – to his amusement, which she shuns and shrinks from as mockery inspired by her appearance, lack of chic; when it's precisely this, her freshness, freckles which attract him.

But, at least, to F.'s amazement and relief, Mother likes him; and F. grateful for time he spends in drawing-room – which

113

releases her to linger longer haying horses. Sneaks back in past drawing-room and upstairs to bedroom and Safety – epitomized in nightly letter to Edward.

This stalemate lasts three years! Then, and in heatwave, Mother plays her most extraordinary card: 'Why don't you go to the cinema with Pierre?' – in front of him, when he hasn't even asked her. And she doesn't want to go, had planned to get child to bed early and take herself for a ride in the cool of the evening.

Goes cinema, nonetheless. And from there to Pierre's bed – with mother in room across the landing *knowing*, herself both in love with Pierre, vicariously sleeping with him, and having revenge on 'upright Englishmen'.

It is June 1944. D-Day. Pierre leaves. They don't expect ever to meet again.

Nightly letter to Edward has lapsed, and continues to do so. Doodle bugs. Sitting in air-raid shelter, Mother for first time opens up to Frances about her own bitter experience of the male.

Frances is filled with remorse for her lack of understanding, now replaced by growing love and admiration. Feels that only she knows what lies behind the mask – the self-discipline, courage, tolerance, loyalty – that no one else could divine these, or the sardonic humour with which Mother has privately viewed the world.

Grown close, they laugh together as Frances has never laughed. On strength of this (taking things more lightly), also news retailed by Gurkha grapevine that Edward has, in India, gone the way of all flesh, Frances now writes confessing her own brief lapse. To her amazement and real dismay Edward replies, via solicitors, that he is instituting divorce proceedings.

Meanwhile – war over – Pierre (supposing F. reunited with Edward) writes Mother to thank for hospitality. Replying, she reveals Edward's move. On F.'s behalf, but unknown to her,

Pierre comes to London where Edward refuses to meet 'French fornicator'.

Pierre now feels free to woo, and Frances easily won. Will marry in England, but plan to live in France, taking Mother – who declines to go. Frances at first refuses to leave her. But Mother adamant – 'managed perfectly well before the war; servants again plentiful, and she may employ Companion'. *Is, in fact, racked by jealousy.*

With Frances distressed on Mother's score, and fraught (as Pierre sees), Mother now cashes in on this; writes to him attributing F.'s nervous state to Edward's getting custody of child if F. goes to live in France. Pierre fights hard, but finally 'honourably' succumbs.

It is he who sends telegram announcing his own death, and – to remove all lines of communication – that of his father, 'only relative', killed with him in car accident.

*

Well, Cool Customer, cooling your heels, it's not bad, better than yours. And I've more substance than you have up my sleeve.

I always fall in love afresh with the P.E. at the station – and out of love on the journey home, as he tells me his news in five minutes. I'm waiting for a feast and get the pickings. He's had extraordinary luck, got all the references (of course I'm thrilled, but he told me over the phone). And Jason has got Giles – off the Shrink, drink? The P.E. says what do I mean, the Shrink? 'But I told you, he and Charlotte. . .'. He's forgotten about the Shrink; but not the drink, which Jason hopes he has solved by extracting Giles from Arabs placing orders for Kleenex at four in the morning – and into a job in the Common Market!

They're all leaving Wimbledon, and going to live where?

When? Are they pleased? How was Giles? Do he and Charlotte seem happier?

The P.E. thinks end of July; and supposes Brussels.

Brussels, oh dear. Well, isn't it all like the Boulevard Haussmann in Paris? The P.E. says but it's worth going for the Brueghels. You don't live in a museum. 'Well, tell me all about the evening with Jason.' I mean *all*. We get as far as *moules marinières*. He's just remembered – they're going to Luxembourg.

Luxembourg! The Moselle. No one could swig whisky when they live in the land of Schloss Bockelheim. Ring to congratulate Giles. They've rented an old farmhouse outside the city in wonderful wooded country.

I'm as happy as Giles sounds sober, will be happy to be on call. Am already happily in the brass bed when the P.E., climbing into this, says: 'By the way, who on earth do you think I saw in London?'

I've no idea. Well after the library and before going on to Wimbledon he'd dropped into the Cavendish for a drink and there was Suzette, deep, so deep in amorous conversation he'd slunk out and back to the pub in Duke Street.

That's marvellous. What was the man like? He couldn't see very well, but lying back says: 'I assume it was Vivers.'

Vivers! No, I've clearly misheard: 'Who?'

'Her cousin. You know, the one who's causing all the trouble.'

'What trouble?'

No answer. He's asleep.

Vivers her cousin! So that's how I know it. The aunt I met was called Vivers. Vivers was the Honourable's maiden name.

But 'causing all the trouble' – then the P.E. knows. . . . He can't. In that case what else can he mean? That Vivers, thick with the Honourable and in on a good thing (Belldale Holiday Homes Limited), is in on kicking Suzette out; and using

116

seductive tactics in order to do so?

In that case why would the P.E. have scuttled back to Duke Street?

Because he agrees about the olive tree.

It doesn't quite wash: if the Honourable can get tied cottages freed by legal methods she doesn't need amorous ones. Possibly with a daughter . . . it wouldn't look good in court. Somewhere around dawn I fall asleep.

And wake late, alone. The P.E. is back in *The Sack*. What does he know? How much does he know? He won't want to talk at lunch. But I can't wait all day – and can say good morning to my husband.

Lure him into our bedroom for a quick cup of coffee, and ask what time he got up, how he slept; then, casually, did I dream it that he saw Suzette in London? No. Well, who is this trouble-making cousin?

'But you know all about it – the one she can't make up her mind to marry because he's simply an English merchant banker.'

I don't know all, in fact a thing about it.

'You must. She talks of nothing else.'

I'm tied here, I don't get to Belldale.

Well, he's told me. Yes, that he's dug her garden.

No, about her hysterics, the time she rolled on the floor and he had to throw cold water over her.

Rolled on the floor. . . . The P.E. threw. . . . I can't believe my ears and can't imagine why he hasn't told me.

He swears he has. I've forgotten. No, he's the dab at forgetting. When he comes in he always goes straight to his study, to cool off, put Belldale out of his mind, get back to his work – and succeeds so well that he has, by the evening, forgotten. Or if he hasn't, puts on some Bach. He's allergic to hysterics. 'Well,' I say now, 'why won't you see she's a wrecker?'

117

The P.E. doesn't take this up. Instead he says, 'Actually I think he's just the man to sort her out.'

I'm on tenterhooks: 'But you haven't met?'

'No. But he's obviously tough and rich. He'd get her out of Paris. I don't think you understand the split in Suzette. You've seen her nesting instinct. She feels she has to write, but also wants to marry and have children. Artistically Vivers isn't a threat, and with his kind of money behind her she would have the freedom to do both.'

Freedom from choice – agonies of. Freedom from money worry. Freedom to write and *live*. No chips please.

'And she'd have a very interesting life. Vivers travels a lot,' the P.E. says, now half-way to the door: Geneva, Washington, South America. . . . There's a Vivers villa (private beach) somewhere outside Rome, but favourite base ranch in Mexico. Kips down Lowndes Square.

'Anywhere else?' I call.

The P.E. puts his head back round the door, laughing: 'Yes, country retreat in Meon Valley.'

'Where's that?'

'In Hampshire. Where exhausted merchant bankers go to fish. Fishing is very relaxing.'

With the Meon Valley up my sleeve, I, too, can afford to relax. Hampshire is a Rolls-Royce roll from London, and Vivers clearly over-housed. His coming here was purely a freak of fancy. He could collect Canalettos, but instead collects beautiful places. By now, having completely forgotten this one, he's probably buying some Cornish Coast to put on his mantelpiece. 'Well no, I've never actually lived in France. . . .' At one time the mere shadow of that voice gave me the shivers. But he hasn't – the poor muff's never *lived* anywhere. The nearest he gets to living is in Mexico and the sooner he carts the Wrecker off there the better.

Meanwhile I'm free to pursue my own line in fishing:

How to get Frances – three years later? – to France. She'll have to be driving a car and taking another woman, who can't be a friend of the bosom. Protégée. Someone she's sorry for who worships the ground F. walks on. Genteel and poor and proud. Art mistress. Initiating F. into Bad Art (lantern-slides). Hearts' desire – to see Switzerland (scraping and saving). F., taken in, offers to drive her there. Doesn't realize mistake till they've crossed Channel. Abroad and at close quarters Emily (?) intolerable. Insists on drinking milk not wine with meals. Hates food, F. revelling in it. Continual scraps over money, as Emily insists on 'paying her way' – one which consists of enjoying nothing. At Reims stays to pray in cathedral, while unregenerate F. sits outside drinking champagne alone!

Then, ten miles from Swiss border, carburettor trouble. Directed back to garage near Besançon. (No sympathy from E., harping on inroads into savings.) F., left to re-route, consulting map, suddenly realizes garage no way from where Pierre had lived. Can't pass so close without seeing this. Inquires at garage for address of the late Colonel Pierre de Saint-Paul. Mechanic nonplussed, says but he's there now.

Though shaken, incredulous, F. unable to resist. And – leaving E. who refuses to budge from car, white with rage at further delay, to wait and fume outside – finds herself, *still inflammably*, faced with Pierre. Also with father in dotage, plus girl who opens door, whom F. at first takes to be a servant, plump, plain, black moustache, now introduced as cousin. Had somehow – how? – assumed Pierre lived in château. House in fact in street leading down to this, former habitation of courtiers or servants?

Explains that Pierre was billeted on them in England during war. Father: 'So you were the fiancée?' Cat out of bag, cousin announces that this was her role from birth. F. tries to reassure

119

her and retreat. But cousin becomes hysterical. F.'s one desire – to bolt. Father chuckling *'C'est mieux que la télévision'*, drama ends with two women in each other's arms. And cousin saying that F. was Pierre's choice. Theirs will be a *mariage de convenance*. He isn't in love with her and must consider himself completely free.

F., nonetheless, emerges devastated and torn. Icy Emily watching now sees Pierre, as, accompanying F. to car, he asks her to stay Besançon hotel, and he will telephone that evening.

F. irresolute. Faith in Pierre shattered. So this is why he defected – but why so cruelly? Why didn't he ever, or simply, tell her of prior engagement? Tries and fails to explain to Emily, who remains impenetrably suffering and silent. This, and F.'s still violent attraction to Pierre, prove decisive. Once again speeding towards Swiss border, F. now, with no explanations and deaf to E.'s protests, turns and heads back to Besançon.

14

A peace which passes all understanding descends when you
put your house in the hands of Messrs Egglestone and Short.
Or so it seems. Mr Egglestone clearly, if not immediately
clearly behind that airforce moustache, is an *esprit fin*. Hushed
and awed he was waiting, hanging on the P.E.'s words as
these, for a week, slide silently on to the page. And for a week
the silence is literally total.

So that I'm taken aback when, on our sixth evening, the
P.E., seeing light I suppose at the end of *The Sack*, suddenly
says:

'How long has the house been on the market?'

Three weeks.

'And we've not had a single bite?'

My answer comes trippingly off the tongue.

Thoughtfully, as if to himself, he says 'That's odd.'

Then that the agents aren't doing their job; he'll give them a
ring tomorrow. He won't, of course, he'll forget. All the same,
I can't risk being caught out; or the risk, which now yawns,
that Egglestone is sitting back on Vivers.

Ring him. He is; and, flattered by Belldale connection, finds it
hard to follow my line of thought – presented as Vivers
unlikely buyer, has enough houses. 'I think you're wrong,
Mrs Gore, I honestly do. But of course, if you wish it, I'll send
you other clients.'

A wrong move. Wrong clients now descend in droves.
Though some, it's true, as chafing I hang around, don't even
descend to descend. One look from the road at my hills and

121

they flee, shaken to their marrows, so fast I can hear the clang of the cattle-grid.

But I'm not always let off so lightly, if you can call it lightly with the fields all pied and smocked, more flowers than grass; and instead of these a couple who've run a fish and chip shop and now aspire to higher things – a Guest House. Pile on snow to no effect. They'll only open in summer. I've been stuck – and it's true – in a snowdrift here in June.

They go, but somehow it's always the same, somehow the day goes with them. What do I do till the P.E. comes downstairs?

Well yes, of course I'm on edge, and of course the P.E. is upset when I burn the stew, *and* break the dish. But two things I can do – whisk round his study during the six o'clock news; and exclude his need to turf out during the day. Additional 'feature': glimpse (glimpse only) of Famous Author at work.

'But I'd have to get up' (references, rug, foolscap).

No, Famous Authors don't; peer briefly through bi-focals, are clearly Deep in Thought and hardly there.

The P.E. tries to be famous and fade, but even at 9 a.m. can't be Deep in Thought if they're coming at twelve. At this rate we'll never get out of *The Sack*, and he finally fades to the pub – if it isn't a Rose by any other name.

Well the Wrecker hasn't rung, hadn't, I took it, returned. Up to now he's always been back within the hour. But it's five o'clock and he's still not here. Cold water, however, and cousins, even cousins named Vivers, are sedatives. He hates missing the news, is sure to be back by six, which is why, on his way up the lane now, he hasn't rung.

He does miss the news. I can still, at a quarter past, sit happily absorbed in my window watching. Only the gulls, gliding, riding the last of the blue gold evening, move. I've never seen the dale so still. Or the walls so clear (I suppose, in fact, it's the sharpness of their shadows). And at half past six can still divert myself – composedly composing an In Memoriam notice: 'The P.E., late of Belldale, sadly missed'.

But by seven my composure has definitely decomposed. And when at half past, half past seven I swear it, the 'phone does finally ring – cold water, my foot! – I let it cuckoo on and cuckold off. N.B. Why are only men not women cuckolded?

Cuckoo. Cuckoo. This time I pick it up.

'Hello. It's me', the Great I Am in that teeny-weeny voice. Isn't, in short, the P., scrap the E.

'We've been trying and trying to ring you.'

Trying? No, meaning to try. *Why hasn't he?*

'We want you to come out to dinner.'

WE – what is the French for *finesse*?

'It's sweet of you, but. . . .

'No, he'll fetch you. He's on his way.'

The assumption, presumption!

'I'm sorry, Suzette, but we can't. He's forgotten we're expecting a call from Mark. It's important. About his Ph.D.'

'Oh. . . .'

'I'd ask you here, but I'm afraid we'll have a lot to discuss.' Well, the last bit's true, it certainly is. 'I'll give you a ring tomorrow and perhaps we can arrange something.'

Arrange to rearrange. 'A marriage has been arranged. . . .' Why, when they aren't any more even in France? Scrub France. I'll give her tapioca pudding. Meanwhile I've exactly fifteen minutes. Pat cushions – you may need these – dust your insouciance. Draw the curtains, Act IV, Scene IV. You've still time to nip upstairs and do something about your hair, and be back on the divan reading – what? Trollop(e), *Can You Forgive Her?* No, put that away. Jane Austen, *Pride and Prejudice*.

The logs blaze and the shadows dance, the car-lights shine through the curtains.

Put down my book and throw him a loving smile. Where on earth have I been? (Where on earth. . . !) Here. Well, he rang at four and again at five. It must have been five to five. I was back at five.

'That's odd. Suzette kept trying and got no answer.'

But he knows when she's high she always gets the code wrong.

I hope it wasn't another cold water session?

No, in fact a champagne one. She'd left a note in the pub to say she was back, clearing out of that cottage and leaving for France tomorrow. So he could hardly not. . . .

No, naturally. . . . Of course not. Quite.

Clearing out! Leaving tomorrow! Though what I'd still like to know is why she leaves notes in the pub and doesn't ring here. Why she confides in the P.E. – if this is what she does. Why I miss out on the champagne.

I am starting, only idly starting to ask these now obsolete questions, but have time to observe that the P.E. (always transparent) is put to it, when the door, as if blown open, frames the Wrecker herself, starry-eyed. A platitude? Well, you try thumbing through *Roget's Thesaurus*; you'll still end up with the star on the Christmas tree.

'Aren't you two ready? I've booked for half past eight.'

Well we're not, it must be said, in silver lamé – a sort of string vest and silver Turkish trousers. As she plops this harem down on the divan the P.E. signals to me a succinct but distinct 'No'.

'But, Suzette, I thought I'd explained about Mark.'

'Oh we must go! We must celebrate.'

Celebrate what? Her imminent departure? If so, I've underrated her sense of irony.

At this delicate point the phone, by some miracle rings. And is by some miracle Mark. As the P.E. answers I hover at his elbow, picking up what I can: 'Good. . . . Good. . . . Excellent. . . . Splendid news. . . . Yes, of course still off the record. Though I can't say I'm surprised. It's certainly an impressive piece of work. There were one or two points I'd

124

like to take up. . . . Well, isn't Pearson at Leeds? Jason could give you a line on Liverpool. Personally I think I'd opt for Leeds rather than Sheffield. . . . But here's your mother, she'd like a word with you.'

'. . . Oh do go to Sheffield! I should so enjoy Louise's reaction: "Isn't that the place where they make knives? So you mean he's really got a proper job at last!"' How, in fact, will he manage for cash in the meanwhile? No problem; he's driving a laundry van. 'But you will have a holiday?' 'Don't worry. I'll send you a card from Torremolinos.' How, though, are we? Has Rome been sacked? The house? No, we haven't sold. A prospective buyer? No, no prospective buyer.

At this point the P.E. ruthlessly confiscates the receiver. Do I want my son to end in the poor-house?

I admit it's a long and for anyone else deadly conversation, the sort where I'd normally say 'I'll ring you back'. Even so I'm startled when, turning from the 'phone, I find Suzette standing on her head.

'Suzette, what on earth are you doing?'

Answer: 'I'm thinking.' No, simply drawing attention to herself. More simply, pickled. I glance at the P.E. who's hitch-hiking with his thumb 'spare room'. So I suppose I'll have to. At least the bed's made up. Between us we get her giggling up the stairs, where, when I've helped her de-lamé and tucked her between the sheets, she's instantly sleeping like a child.

The next morning she's gone. Gone gone for ever. Despite this the P.E. doesn't work well. I'm not surprised. He's exhausted, and, with his train of thought in shreds, clients are as nothing to Belldale havoc. Well at least we'll have no more of that. And if since then, in the evenings, I might as well have married the man in the moon, he did, when he got off the train, say with luck a week. Translated from the *couleur de rose* tongue the P.E. wags this should mean a fortnight – which is now. Any day as I stand at the sink his arms will again go round me, and he'll say 'Could you put that parsnip down a moment?'

But if so and if silent, why isn't he more cheerful? Ask him. He's keeping something from me. I can always tell. He's going to say 'I didn't want this to happen. But I'm afraid I am in love with Suzette.' Instead he says 'Sweetheart, you're as white as a sheet!' Then that in five days he's written and sacked one page. The relief!

All the same why is he blocked? Take myself off to the pike; and think can he really be pining for the Wrecker? Well how else explain it? It's a perfect day, the scree in points, white bunting along the fells as, russet and blue, these rush down as if rushing into the sea – a rush that usually fills me with such joy. But not today. And it's not the Wrecker, not just *The Sack*, not the uncertainty of where we'll go. It's a feeling I don't know how to define. I suppose . . . I suppose it's loneliness.

But I've never been lonely.

And never been so estranged from the P.E. We're both living alone side by side. Why? Because he, of the two of us, is the more deeply disturbed. Why can't we discuss our common troubles?

It was he, after all, who produced those incriminating fuel bills. He was the one who said we had to sell. Yes, but you can't write under threat. He thought he'd be through with the book. Answer: remove immediate threat.

Yes, go home and ring Egglestone. I'm taking the house off the market? No, simply taking no clients for two weeks.

The release, the release! And hay-time! And a heatwave! Woken at five by Tom's tractor under the window. With a white rose reef of mist still running the length of the dale – how can Tom possibly know? Well, he does. So I head for my study and draft? No, I'm heading for oblivion. 'Whenever we

126

unconsciously feel we live' if that means anything, and, with all respect to E. Bowen, I'm bound to say I don't see how it can. So I'll leave you – well, whoever you are you're useful – to work at it, and head for that strange halo around Lobb's House, the colour of orange and yellow plums with – I can't unravel this either – somehow the implication of purple plums. Not apricots or peaches. But one never thinks of fruit here. The idea is too fruity for these hard hills.

Already it's hot enough to bask. It's going to be a scorcher. And everywhere, near and far throughout the dale, the purring, churning of tractors. It's like a hive of bees. Won't it, though, disturb the P.E.? No, not after jungle warfare. It's like the vacuum cleaner – life going on, a reassuring sound.

Return to the house for my bathing dress, and look into his study. And yes, his hand is moving across the page. Up to the moor; sheep, even shorn sheep, huddled panting in whatever shade the beck affords. Stretch out and blot out, only lark sounds pirouetting. 'Whenever we unconsciously feel we live.'

Well this is as near as I'll get to it, smelting my self down, shrinking the circumference of my being to two red discs laid over my eyes, inscribed, if I watch these, with changing blue hermetic hieroglyphs.

Lie there with larks for thoughts, forgetful, self-forgotten. It's quite a feat. Perhaps I could even arrange to have my self burnt to a cinder, and – experience, temperament, patterns imposed by the past and dictating the future – extinguished, rise like a phoenix from the ashes. Well, it would certainly help. And the P.E.?

I sit up, suddenly urgently needing to know what's happening behind that window that's behind his head.

It's deliciously cool in the house, like a larder. And nothing in the larder; nothing but soup! And it's *twelve* o'clock. It can't be. Yes, there are different kinds of time. A child's day is as long as twenty of mine. How did the clock get changed? I can

127

still put it back. I can have enough, great bales of time if I leave the cloth whole and don't rip it into rags – as Montherlant but no one else explains. Everyone else is killing time. This is what changed the clock, wound up to tick so fast they wouldn't hear. And they don't, of course; don't ever hear its great gold resonance spreading like the ripples in a pond.

Meanwhile it won't kill me to make a potato salad. But first just a 'client's' glimpse round that study door. He doesn't so much as glance up, and when he comes downstairs merely says that his pen is liquefying. In other words even here in the house that Papermate pen is flowing, in other words the ice is melting at last.

At one, Tom's back in the field, the hay spinning behind him in spirals, dandelion clocks, green spider's webs. Rose, too, now is there with her wooden rake, pulling it out from the walls, doggedly never pausing – killing time, or living, working and living? Already there are blisters forming on her small hard-worked hands; and 'Bye,' she says, 'sum caider would be luvely.' Tom, joining us, says 'Bye it's hot in tractor!' A Tom so changed I barely recognize him as the dark, tense man I know with grooves in his face. Though I've seen this Tom before, in Provence, in the Greek islands. Tom, it's plain, doesn't know what's hit him. Burnt down to the burning moment, body and mind fused, he's one with himself, at peace as never before.

'Dear Mrs Jones, yes, it's true what you've heard. Our exact address is unclear. But *Poste Restante*, the Here and Now, will find us.'

Poste Restante 9 p.m. Look out through my letter-box. At last they're having supper under the trees.

Below the field, tossed once more, lies in long green plaits. Between these – how? – it's already the colour of corn. Tomorrow they'll bale, package it up and the whole of that great meadow will slide like Christmas parcels into the byre, the loft of a byre so small you wouldn't think it could. Well, isn't it like the covers of a book?

I hope it's like a book. I think the P.E.'s baling (out). I hope Rome's starting to look like a shorn sheep. For that's what the shorn field looks like, as sheepish, meek and foolish. But wait, the rooks are coming from Westminster. What do they do all day down there since they only arrive in the evening, and it's here in this field that they hold their parliament, always in the same place, always under the ash-tree? I can't help suspecting they've come from the Old Bailey.

Well, what do I do all day? Sip champagne like the Wrecker, sip the champagne of days that can't possibly last. Yes, they can; you've said so. An hour can contain ten hours. You can afford to go to your study and draft.

15

Where was I – am I? Half here and half in Besançon – not, in other words, in the Here and Now. *Poste Restante*. . . . Come, come, Mrs Gore, this will never do. You're here to be helped. Just lie back, shut your eyes, relax, shut out the blue of the sky, and what do you see? The sky. No, a bill from you, Mr Harley Street Quack (quack quack).

Yes of course you hate me today, Mrs Gore. But keep looking straight ahead and you see, don't you, a telephone box? At least let's hope it's a box and not one of those hotel helmets, as otherwise Emily will be listening, and if she is will overhear Frances talking to Pierre and arranging to meet him the following evening in Dijon (a meeting clearly impossible for Pierre in his own district).

Emily, livid and *Lesbian*, will have to be put on a train, return fare paid by F. to Lake Lucerne.

I find, in fact, I've grown fond of and am sorry to part with Emily. Why? I suppose because she's real, arrived by herself like a mushroom, grew and wasn't contrived – as are Frances and Pierre?

Yes, I should instantly pick out Emily in a bus queue. Whereas Frances I recognize less and less.

I've never really seen Pierre. No, perhaps it's important not to. But how much does your sudden attachment to Emily stem from the fact that the outcome of Dijon is painfully obvious? The truth is I shrink from describing erotic love?

You can't have read Flaubert's directions: Treatment as for denim. Transferred to paper should always be well shrunk.

Flaubert makes Henry Miller's antics look like good clean fun. May I not be confusing sex with love? They are, aren't they, vaguely linked? Yes, *I am jumping at shadows*. At last the point's sunk in! Emily's point.

Shadows into substance: 'Seeing other people as shadows, oneself as the only reality.' Also (source? I've lost it, no matter) something to the effect that such shadows are often menacing. Stick to the point. I am. That's just what I'm doing and why – why I'm stuck with somehow sticking this out.

Come, come Mrs Gore. Relax, close your eyes. You actually saw Frances in the flesh, saw the girl in the woman, and through Edward, via *Sole Colbert*, saw to Pierre; saw Frances with Pierre at a table laid with a plain check cloth, eating *crustacés*, drinking Macon Blanc – and, don't tell me, 'lost to all but each other'. Before I know where I am we'll have 'locked in each other's arms'. I knew, I've always said this would end in tears.

Head for Left Luggage (alias the reader's lecherous imagination). Well, it's high time someone else did some work, helpful (attention all shipping) at least to posit a reader who will not only serve as cited above, but supply one with *terra firma*, allow one time off duty to get one's metaphors well and truly mixed – muddled, garbled, mazed, *to lose the thread*, and

> . . . all, all in a rout,
> Thy chase had a beast in view

in a raight mess guaranteed to fettle one up.

I will now stop beating about the bush, in fact a labyrinth the clue to which lies in the reader's hand. Feed him some rope and (bearing in mind Jason's bill of fare) leave him to find his own way through the maze.

From here the rope will lead and leave you some twenty miles short of Avallon, where, so torrential and blinding is the

131

rain, the lovers decide to pull off at the first *auberge* they see. And Pierre is paged.

How? By whom? Frances feels a first sudden uneasiness, not wholly dispelled by Pierre's explanation: he has always to let H.Q. (Intelligence) know his whereabouts, and had himself placed the call. She fails to shake off the feeling that Pierre has in some way deceived her. He has never, when they've signed in, said 'I've booked a room', staying, she had always thought, where the spirit moved them. And so, Pierre says, they have; he hasn't booked. But in that case why has he never said '*Il faut que je téléphone,*' still less done so in her presence? Pierre says:

'How serious we are!' As Frances is, and remains so, Pierre lights a cigarette; then, leaning back and blandly crossing his legs (yes, I've just realized. Of course! That's why I've never seen Pierre – *he's Vivers*) says there may be state secrets she shouldn't hear. Frances thinks: 'Of course. I've never thought of that. He's really a spy. Like the Gestapo.'

But at Avallon (*Hotel de la Poste*) it befits you to eat in silence, and at the end of the meal to order *marc*. Pierre orders *marc*, and at last the silence is broken. He is asking Frances to marry him.

And then? Well then there is *Calvados*. And then? Well, Rouen of course. And then? Look, don't you ever do it yourself?

Well trot off. I'm drafting not writing, and all I need to say here is that nothing remains of the old Frances. Even the once lank Titian hair, blowing across her face as she sits in the passenger seat, seems other, thicker, freshly aflame, alive.

They are nearing Le Havre and happily discussing exact date of wedding (Pierre will require three weeks to make his arrangements), when he suddenly alters course: why not here, in Le Havre, by special licence?

Frances, flustered – car-ferry booked – demurs on Mother's account.

132

Pierre says they'll stop at next café and talk it out. Meanwhile he drives on, silent now, absorbed in his own thoughts and, apparently failing to see oncoming car, swerves violently into high wall (passenger side). Frances, thrown through windscreen, escapes with shock and cuts. But has narrowly escaped death.

That fills the bill for today, Mr Quack. Your charges are high for boredom. Well, I've bored myself almost to extinction. I don't want to see ahead, what I want is not to. I certainly don't – who does? – want to see a telephone box.

You came to me to be cured, Mrs Gore. It's all here in your notes: 'Cured of Guesswork, of Reading Herself into Others; patient requires to be smelted down and rise again like the phoenix.' But what if I rose in the likeness of Louise? With convictions made of concrete, seeing nothing but telephone boxes and Duty and flower arrangements? I'm off to the beck.

Nuts on the hazel already, the rowans thick with berries – why, in July, when the birds won't need them for months? Or is it an old wives' tale, this portending a hard winter? A hard winter – now, what would that mean?

Later, when it's cooler, I'll go down to see the bellflowers. For years I looked in the flower book under white. Not till the P.E. insisted that my willow-herb was loosestrife (which it was) did I find them under mauve. But to me their candles will always glimmer whitely in the wood.

One should still know they are really mauve.

I don't see why.

Accuracy is first cousin to truth. What if the P.E. got his facts wrong? But aren't there different kinds of fact, of truth, accuracy? This is one of your sillier questions to date. Telephone boxes are red – and fields, Mr Quack, are green? But the one into which I now drop through a stile in the wall is blue, midnight blue. It's scabious, still dark in colour, only in mid-July coming out.

Hazels take back your nuts, rowans hoard your beads. Haven't you heard what the grouse, perched on the walls, are saying, 'G' back, g' back'? Yes, they're foolish birds. Well, have you never pondered the oddness of it – that everyone walks obediently through life in one direction, all with their noses pointing the same way?

Even the seasons are cast – don't tell me – in narrative form. Stop quacking! Go back to whatever you were for me, beck.

For my part, meanwhile, I'm going back to the house. At least I thought I was. But I'm not. I'm going back to the P.E. I can't believe my eyes. He's outside digging the garden, outside digging our garden – we're out of *The Sack*.

16

Woken in the night by rain lashing the window. It's odd to lie there exulting; but I do. And am disappointed when, at seven, I get up to nothingness, from upstairs nothing, it seems, but a grey whiteness. Below, though, Lord the drama! All walls black as coal, walls made of wet black shining coal; cows eating, larches tossing, the ash-tree going ho-ho, one wall like a scimitar taking a Pegasus leap – all there, but all else, everything around as doom-dark as if we're going to have *Macbeth*.

We're not, though, going to have it. The P.E.'s still in bed but awake, drinking coffee, reading the post – which includes a card from Mexico: the Wrecker's married Vivers and is ecstatic about her new home. The P.E., as he said before, thinks it a good thing. For my part this is an understatement. She's baled out at last from our lives and Vivers be thy name (hers) for ever and ever, Amen.

Meanwhile I'll have to ring Egglestone. The P.E. says 'Need we?' Naturally. What he needs is a thorough rest. It's Tuesday. Line up Egglestone, say, for next Monday. Why line him up? Why not wait? Anyone would think I was hot for certainties. Am I? No, it's just that there's thunder about.

Also in the evenings the news, then Handel, Haydn. Music is always his medicine. He's snoozed all day, but still says 'Let's have an early night', sleeps late – in other words is dog-tired, still too tired to talk. And it's not that I'm desperately waiting to talk, to plan where we might live – the concept 'Future' has become meaningless to me.

In fact by Friday I find I'm uneasy, suspicious of all this snoozing. How do I know he's not lying there racking his brains? Is his study, in any case, the wisest place to lie? Isn't that day-bed, perhaps, like St Lawrence's gridiron? Couldn't we go away, I plead, just for a couple of nights? In this weather? No, but if it breaks?

It doesn't break. And I briefly make do with the sycamores, six days ago sultry and dark, glaucous, ominous, stranded amidst the alien corn which is of course alien here, merely stubble braised by the long heat.

So that this morning crossing the field, bound for the beck in spate, with already the sound of its goldrush in my ears, filling my mind, I'm unprepared for sycamores lacquered and shining, each leaf lacquered and shining, more shining than green.

My mistake lies in walking on. There's a car drawn up in the lane, drawn up where they always draw up to admire the view (transistors, magazines), the valley wending below (valley not dale) pastoral, idyllic, green. *All of it green.* Too green, pastoral, English for my taste. With two days to go I'll be thankful when Monday comes round.

Meanwhile with all to clean this will dispose of Sunday (*dispose* of a day that will no more return to this earth than that on which Pepys walked out and saw the baker's house in Pudding Lane 'where the late great fire begun'!). In fact there's only our half to clean, flick round rest with a duster. Can't help wishing we could have kept on the drawing-room. Sit in the window – there's nothing to see. Even the rain's green. But it's bigger, more peaceful in here than the other room.

Look up at the fireplace, the sweep of its curve, that great stone surround – no tasteful pine, no possible place for Dresden. And think, Lord! how I've missed it – missed what exactly? Its stillness, of course; a certain largesse, exemption, exoneration – I suppose I'm arriving at charity. Its span spanning my life, my death, it demands nothing of me. I think, 'can a fireplace grant you absolution?'

There's also the fact, I suppose, that I've never worked in here, that this was the room we came to when work was over, still retaining for me its old repose. Steeped in this my eyes rove idly round the room, idly aware of past and present as merging, gathered but loosely like wild flowers held in a child's hand: the chair which once stood in solitary satinwood state in our one-time otherwise naked marble hall; the diamond glitter, even on a day as dark as this, of my grandmother's Waterford fruit-salad bowl, which, if tapped, emits a deep Big Ben, long-lingering chime.

I'm round to the marquetry table, its barley-sugar legs held together by clamps and in consequence cheap, which when we first married stood at the foot of our bed, now holding a lamp to read by on the sofa. By all means draw your conclusions; they aren't my conclusions.

It's only now that I actually notice something, something small and white, a card lying on the table. It must have dropped out of those flowers the P.E. brought me that day when the Wrecker was coming to dinner and I thought. . . . Amused by the recollection of my wrath, I get up and drift over to reread the message on it. The peace shatters like glass: it's a visiting card! Vivers's card, the one he left, I suppose, as I ushered him out. At the time I never so much as glanced at it. It must have slipped under the salver. I'd forgotten its existence. But even if it finally slid to the floor behind the table, nothing explains its flight now across the room.

There's been no one in the house this week.

Except the P.E.

But in that case, if he picked it up, why didn't he bring it to me, and say 'How on earth did this get here?' Because he simply assumed the Wrecker had dropped it? Or because, being the P.E. with his mind on other things, he picked it up

137

without looking at it. He couldn't have read it anyway without his spectacles. So that I can't think why I'm worrying.

I'm not. I've simply stood mechanically tearing it up, then, finding the fragments in my hand, walked through and put these in the fire. We still, in July, need and have one in the other room.

You can't burn a ghost.

I'm not. I'm burning my lies.

'Patient requires to be smelted down and rise again like the phoenix' – this morning, more like, very like an owl. Well, for days it's been too dark to see or guess the time. But this morning the bedroom's already up and awake, filled with a daffodil brightness. Still in bed pull back the edge of the curtain – and it *is* blue not green out there, a sky with the promise of bluebells, blue hills at the head of the dale, but opaquely blue, and below there's no mist, all clear, the small white-windowed houses as small and happy and neat as calico print. Smoke from chimneys going straight up, already there's washing out. Monday! Of course it's Monday. Monday at last.

Restored to my Real Estate role – caretaker, undertaker – I go to the door wearing my rue with a difference, hungry for faces, any faces. Each one tells a story. The stories walk in. One day I'll write them down.

But how do you write this one? Prim, immensely correct, elderly man, waistcoat, Savile Row (price of last suit, shocking fit, went to law about it), with youthful buxom mistress – *gym mistress*! Wrong; in Sotheby's; expert on was it Tanagra or Cinquecento? She must have been dull if I can't, and I can't remember. Dull, healthy, in no way 'with it', still less *simpatico*. But practical. Yes, I suppose that must be it – why I draw a blank; she's never lost a thing, never lost her pen,

138

lost her way, hasn't got a soul to lose. So why do I give her a thought? Because I want to remember, not forget.

This is a complicated matter I won't go into here, except to say that once I knew a man who could remember not just the plot, but the flavour, beauties, failings, sentences from a book he'd read at fifteen – and tried all his life to write, and couldn't; and died of drink. A faultless memory is a fearful thing. Because, don't you see, if you can't forget there's nothing rich and strange to rise up from the bottom of the pond? Which is both a consoling doctrine if your memory's a sieve like mine, and why I don't propose to forget the girl.

But here the mystery thickens. They're both dead nuts on the place, determined to buy, though not in any hurry. He's planning to retire here. When are we planning to leave? We aren't. No plans. A survey? Naturally. Give us the treatment ('not in a hurry', delays, Savile Row), and they think they'll knock us down, the P.E. says. He's right, of course. But where and when did my husband, I'd like to know, come by this sudden shrewdness, this wordly wisdom?

Not that it matters. I'd much prefer to sell to Mr Morse, the nice auctioneer who, over the years, has sold us up bit by bit – first those 'Attic' vases we bought in Dieppe (in a rabbit-skin shop in Le Pollet, in our long-ago junketing days), the Rockingham tea-set which wasn't, it turned out, quite all it should be (wedding-present from my near and dear), pictures the P.E. has never ceased to regret. And then, last year, the chest of drawers, the same chest of drawers in which an attempt was once made to make me be tidy; where instead, in vain, I buried novels with promising titles which I hoped would teach me all about love (as opposed to the book about babies, in fact bees and pollen). Drawers which later held my gilded youth.

Quick, quick read to the children; Jehovah's Witnesses; where

139

are my earrings, into my evening dress and downstairs already the hum of voices in the drawing-room; that venison can't *still* be tough – it is. Back upstairs with fruit jelly, a treat. Alice goes on reading. How old do I think she is? Too old for jelly. Hers isn't, it's chocolate mousse. She gives me a brief cool look. Night and day – one day she'll be the one. Mark sits up: night is day! But where is Giles, I ask? He's not in his room. No, Giles is in the playground beating up little Lucy whose mother is now on the doorstep to tell me so. Oh Giles, Giles, why tonight? Because I'm having a party. Because . . . well it's all there in the chest of drawers.

Wasn't I once going to write a story called *The Chest of Drawers*? Yes, but not that story. Something about finding something out, something about my pristine, foolish, gilded, gelded youth. Your children don't allow for that; no. Alice wanted a mother who was fat, fixed up and knitting. Well I've never been able to knit, and there's no point now.

It's over to you, Mr Morse. And I really think it is, as I try not to gape at Mrs Morse, or perhaps I should say at this unsuspected aspect of Mr Morse whom I've always before met in official guise. Though I should, I suppose, have spotted it then – that the black overcoat had a good deal more *je ne sais quoi* than the P.E.'s, and, hands in pockets, was worn with a manner to match; that, discreet as was the effect, the shirt had wide *pink* stripes (shirt made to measure, if not Jermyn Street). Men's shoes are – a mystery – the acid test; I didn't notice these, but don't doubt they would have walked him into White's.

Officially ageless – old, thought I! – somewhat like a mole, in so far as his features surfaced at all; more like, very like the grandest sort of butler, impersonal, correct, anonymous; the old-fashioned type of expert, in more senses than one still in the service of the antique world.

140

And now here I am not only with a Mr Morse in jeans, collar, no tie, who can't be a day over forty, goodlooking, bronzed, attractive, but with a glamorous, several-years-younger-than-Alice Mrs Morse. Slim green-stockinged legs in green knickerbockers, removing – 'May I' – her cloak, deer-stalker hat, giving her boyish Vidal Sassoon all it needs, a shake, and warming pearl-pale hands before the fire. Lord, how I've yearned for a cloak! Also knickerbockers. Also – I know, I'm sorry – a deer-stalker hat. 'Brightness falls from the air, Queens have. . . .' I didn't quite catch. . . . Nothing. It's just that I find I don't yearn any more.

And it's not that I don't enjoy the cut of Mrs Morse's jib. But somehow the chic does act as a barrier. Or perhaps it's the cool. I feel a bit as I do with Alice's friends, as if though present I'm absent, not even a ghost.

Elegance is, however, in my eyes desirable, self-possession likewise, cool merely a concept they think they've invented – either better than mateyness which I dread like the foul fiend. And in this the Morses are different from Alice's friends – 'I'm John', 'Call me Anne' – whose identity, lacking their surnames, I never – of course it hurts Alice – succeed in learning.

Formally, gradually does it. There are shades of intimacy. And although for once the story doesn't walk in, I'm selling my house and actually glad that it doesn't – with reservations. It's cleaner this way.

I don't want to be embroiled with those who inherit my life here, don't want a glimpse of what lies behind the façade, am grateful for my client's enigmatic detachment – with, as I've said, reservations. Does her self-possession, for instance, leave room for dispossession? Is there a crack, any chink in that tweed chainmail through which the sky might filter its confusion, paraphernalia? There's also the question of striped umbrellas; may she not import these and lay on dry martinis

141

before lunch? No, the gales will blow the umbrellas down; Mr Morse has a palate, also a cellar, and only drinks vintage wines.

If I've any further doubts, those chic knickerbockers have climbed – and I bet you haven't – Wild Boar Fell.

No, my mind's made up.

'Made up'?

How do you 'make up your mind'?

Wait, wait I'm on the brink of something. On the brink of selling my house?

No, of something I've thought before without understanding. Something that's been at the back of my mind (mental spinal chord, slopping about between its slipped discs?), something about making it up as you go; changing as you go through life *as if you'd made it up*.

Meaning I've grown out of knickerbockers?

Well, if that's all. . . ! It isn't. I won't have 'my mind made up' by Alice, Morses, age or anything else. Don't you want to go all through life, the whole gamut of human experience? Through grief, being crippled, senile, blind? No.

I thought you were hot on reality.

One waxes hot and cold.

If you'd only take it more quietly you might see – what? That this has its positive side: 'And we shall be changed!' as *The Messiah* joyfully proclaims.

Well, isn't that what you've always wanted, are terrified you won't be? Don't you see that we have to go through the fire?

If you mean, as Louise puts it, 'We're given the strength, etc. Amen,' I can't take that sort of talk.

If only you'd try to keep calm you might see what you've started to see. Yes, I was starting. . . . What was I starting to see?

That I make up my face not my mind. That my life *is* like a fiction, in fact made up for me as I go along. That you aren't invited, you're ordered to line up for Golders Green, and you don't whisk through that furnace in half an hour.

Listen, think back, back to the day when you lay in the sun on the moor. You did, you know, express a desire for cremation. To quote: 'I might even arrange to have myself burnt to a cinder. . . .'

I wish I'd never invented that blasted phoenix.

But don't you see that it all adds up? I don't want to add it up. You don't hold with Forster's 'connect, only connect'? No, I don't want to connect. I want to disconnect. I'd always stick to bricks without the mortar. In fact a dry-stone wall; you can see through the chinks.

I don't want to know what it means to 'make up your mind'.

The truth is I know quite well what it means. That's just the trouble. Well, time out of mind you've something on your mind, if you're not actually out of your mind: Have you seen Mrs Gore in her mind lately? What frame of mind? Oh, the usual. Can't think what she sees in a window.

'You ought to see my cucumber frames this year.'

17

Mrs Gore has 'decided' to sell to Mr Morse. Mr Gore has offered no objections, beyond the fact that this may entail the concurrence of Mr Morse. Both meanwhile are now back in their studies, Mrs G. making heroic efforts not to see and not to say there's a cloud like a cucumber. Mr G. doesn't see the cloud. He's just seen the electricity bill and is lying back with his eyes closed. Below, at the foot of the dale, unseen by both, the road winds on, the road which leadeth unto life. 'Well, plenty of people, I know, can do without Yorkshire, but you'll not see a man look more in need of a nice big cut from our sirloin and one of my gooseberry pies you were on about. . . .

'Mrs Gore does her best, I'm sure. But did you read the last one! You'd not make telly out of that. She's on with another now, and from what she's told me I must say it sounds a bit more like. The heroine's called Frances and she's just been out in France. But what with Frances and France I get confused. You'd think she'd see it and change the names because it's half her trouble – you do get confused with Mrs Gore. You'll likely not mind that Mrs Jones – as went to Harrogate, yes – well she once said something ever so queer: thought the books were meant to be confusing. And it's come to me now that she could've read an early one, a whodunit, because this new one is a mystery story.'

Yes, wrapped in mystery, as impenetrably wrapped as the

cheese we get if we don't drive fifteen miles. Well, I still can't see the end.

No, you've learnt to live without one, concocted a sort of convenient amnesia. But ends do happen, and when they do they're not so different from stiles, or gates: you climb over and go on.

With our noses all obediently pointing the same way.

Would you *like* people to live for ever?

No, heaven forbid. Yes, a select few.

It's four days. . . . Egglestone still hasn't rung.

Ends – ends and means. The means to point your nose in the direction of sun, sea, vineyards, figs. Cicadas. Olives. *You* could write in an olive grove. You could write like Lermontov in an olive grove.

To get there go via drawing-room in Richmond, where Frances now lives with Mother. Drawing-room transferred intact, still Indian jungle, still lit only by same small lamp drooping its light on cards behind which Mother sits, still sits in her lair.

Lair now in literal sense – where everything conspires to prevent Frances, returning radiant, from detecting any change. Gaily: 'Who do you think. . . ?' She hadn't even been able to get the words out; will never, she thinks, to dying day forget small figure rising, *standing* (she can't!), white knuckles gripping chair, and trembling as if with palsy from head to foot with rage. And F. had thought she would be so happy, so thrilled. . . !

Emily, of course, has got in first. And Mother flies at Frances uttering words F. didn't know she knew. . . . How could she so demean herself with a common liar? Frances, herself now infected with the ague, fails (is hardly equipped) to convince her he hadn't lied – or betrayed an inkling of the truth. But by her transparent horror, shock, palpable ignorance, does allay fear behind Mother's fury.

F. now free to give own extended version of Emily's story: the meeting with Pierre, his father, the cousin-fiancée; scene which ensued – one Mother seems thoroughly to enjoy. And the château, what was it like? It wasn't a château, as F. had herself, she admits, been surprised to find. But why, how had they ever formed impression that it was one – if not because Pierre had so often mentioned this, describing it with affection and expressly as *chez moi*?

F., who has given château no further thought and is only, drawn out by Mother, recalling events swiftly and wholly consumed by what followed these, now finds herself freshly nonplussed. Hadn't his letters of old, too, been headed simply '*Le Château*', hers addressed not to a number nine but to a hamlet, Montrouge-le-Château, trickling down a hill and far too small to require a street number? Its name, and Pierre's diminutive '*Le Château*', explained the confusion.

Mother remains dissatisfied: 'But when he was billeted on us he often and always described an actual château – the gates, an avenue, the park; I can see the rooms.'

Frances suddenly feels oddly relieved. Because there had been a château, of course, where doubtless he'd played as a child, though clearly he'd talked to Mother more about this. And it would for a child in that poky house have been a paradise, home rather than a second home.

It came back to her now: 'The owner's quite young, Pierre's age, but a cripple.'

'Oh, did you meet him?'

'Hardly in Dijon, Mother!'

(She's disappointed. She wants some proof of Pierre's veracity. For my sake. Naturally . . . after last time.)

Next day proof comes in letter, passionate love-letter, first read by Frances at breakfast in Mother's presence; but oddly,

146

awkwardly containing no message for her, beyond, in postscript: 'Remember me to your mother.' Frances translates this: 'He sends his love and says he's writing to you.' Retires bedroom with letter to read, re-read, and write her own: 'PS. Do, if you can, write Mother a line.' Slips out to letter-box and back, glancing into drawing-room – Mother absorbed in own passionate pursuit. Frances inspects store-cupboards. Returns drawing-room with sherry. Mother still doesn't look up, finishes game. Then, having so far said nothing, sipping her sherry, says:

'How did . . . did Pierre never explain his "death"?'

Frances, calmly: 'Of course. Our first evening together. Apparently French Intelligence intervened.' Describes his being, as she'd thought, mysteriously paged, her sudden, persistent uneasiness on learning that, unknown to her, he had all along kept in touch with H.Q.

'He'd never dreamt that I'd think he'd been hiding this from me. Naturally. To him it was simply a routine military duty. And they were, after all, Secret Service calls.'

Mother says nothing; then wryly: 'Yes, possibly. Or possibly secret calls to the fiancée.'

The fiancée! That poor girl! Whom Frances had likewise forgotten and who had deserved better of her. But F. for once is confident; laughs: 'It probably was the fiancée! That was the night he asked me to marry him.'

Letters come almost daily from Pierre, but somehow, despite these, Frances increasingly restless and indecisive, withheld by feeling of superstition from starting to sort or pack. Nor is her heart in shopping for a trousseau. But finally screws herself up and one bright blowing day sets off reluctantly – and buys hat for wedding. Renewed by outing, in buoyant mood twirls around in hat for Mother's approval: yes, it's extemely becoming.

That evening Mother, laying out cards, looks up: 'Have you

never thought that he intended to murder you in that car?'

No, of course not. Why should she? What would have been the point? The cousin presumably has a sizeable *dot*? Perhaps, but he was perfectly free. By now such questions are powerless to trouble her. With only a week to go and Pierre confirming arrival – date, train, time he will hope to be with them – even impending separation from Mother is mitigated. Close friend lives in next street and through her F. obtains housekeeper whom Mother calmly accepts. F. would be hurt, were she not relieved, by Mother's seeming indifference, one further instance of her iron will, culminating towards end in almost total withdrawal. F., too, now finds herself shunning drawing-room, and evading battle Mother is clearly waging. The darkened room, where only sound is that of cards being turned, puts her unbearably on edge. Cannot but feel her happiness as infringement, desecration – on par with summer sunlight flooding in.

But on day itself Mother rises to occasion, gaily insists that since Pierre will arrive around six, they should greet him in evening dress. Has for some time dispensed with ritual of changing for dinner. Now, as F. helps her to do so, and says 'You look like the bride!', Mother reveals that this was her wedding dress.

Table is laid, whole salmon already on sideboard covered with muslin, as clock, invisible on mantelpiece, chimes six, half-past six, seven, half-past seven. At nine, Mother retreats behind Patience cards. There's been some hitch, he's sure to ring: F.'s own train had been late. But not, close on midnight, as late as this.

And so that night they wait, wait up, wait on for the throb of a taxi. . . .

For Frances the real wait is a longer one.

Two years later, and then not for two months after Mother's death – playing Patience and slumping over cards – can F. face

148

entering bedroom, finality of loss implicit in sorting, disposing of Mother's clothes.

Tortoiseshell brushes and powder bowl still on dressing table; face still surely mockingly in mirror. F.'s feeling suddenly one less of loss than guilt, profanation. Works quickly, like thief, through wardrobe, chest of drawers, everywhere haunted by Mother's scent. Unexpected relief of desk, most dreaded task: scentless, legal, insurance papers, all methodically filed; bottom drawer packets of letters from India; small drawers in which she'd kept sealing wax, labels, paper clips. . . .

And, under labels, two letters from Pierre.

With no thought now of profanation sinks down on bed to read these. Both, to her disappointment, six years old. Both incomprehensible. And addressed to Mother care of Hortense, the friend, her lifelong friend in next street, then at Couden. But why on earth sent care of Hortense?

Because letters form part of long correspondence – in which Mother had worked to prevent marriage.

Shock great. Too great to accept. F. ends by rejecting this. Hortense will be able to explain.

But most Hortense, old, secretive, will say: 'Well, of course, Adèle never thought him suitable for you.'

Suitable! But Mother herself had been devoted to Pierre.

'Hortense, were there other letters . . . last time?'

Hortense – eyes like small black beads – says no need for letters 'because your mother knew it wouldn't come off.'

Knew! When she'd dressed up that night – *and in her own wedding dress*. No, Hortense is too old, isn't all there.

Besides how, what could Mother have known? That Pierre was dishonourable? Or honourable and would honour long-standing engagement? But had honour prevented him writing to tell her so?

149

Perhaps the Indian letters aren't all Indian. That night Frances sits up searching through these for one in Pierre's hand, some message. None comes. Or none she can immediately decode.

A message does, however, come in the Indian letters themselves as, by 3 a.m., half-awake, she falls to mechanically reading – and facing, forced at last to face, inexorable truth of her father's words:

'You accuse me of unfaithfulness. But to what am I unfaithful? To your own inherent destructiveness, the destructive use you make of your beauty, your cruel lust for power, your hatred of happiness, your will to destroy.'

Won't that wash, do as an end?

You can't have two letters running. And there is, of course, another letter.

In that case it will have to go in. But often things won't. They destroy the rhythm of your sentence, balance of section, chapter, book? George Eliot managed. Teutonically.

If you can't fit things in, you will have to learn to. As with unpalatable facts. Life isn't a poem. No. And a book is a book is prose – no rose.

Well, if that's how you feel why not clear off to the beck, leaving a gap? If you don't fill this in someone else will. Someone else will anyway. Practically no one reads what one actually writes. They all read into the book what they want. Take Lowry's *Fall of the House of Usher* (far better than Poe's). Well, I've checked with Poe and it's not there, any of it – no doctor, to whom narrator reads; no 'Mrs' Usher; no 'flames licking . . . along the carpets'; *no house on fire* 'falling to pieces all around them'. Why? Because Lowry has not only been through the fire, lives with his 'house' falling to pieces around him, but has actually twice had his own house burnt down.

And been told that he looks rather like Poe.

So having inserted gap, symbolizing GAP, decent interval, leave it to Mabel-the-daily:

'Here's a letter for you, Miss Frances,' come as Frances briefly, with pounding heart, assumes by second post. In fact found by Mabel, repapering Mother's drawers. And two years old; but two is better than six. Dated and stamped *par Exprès* – in that case here in house at least four days before night when they'd waited up. . . . Opened and read, intercepted out of charity, malice, triumph?

And yes he had wanted to kill them both in that car. '. . . Why, why wouldn't you marry me then, in Le Havre as I asked you to? I felt in my bones that it otherwise wouldn't come off. Your excuse was your mother. I knew her hold on you. And bear in mind that I'd lost you to her once. I'm not superstitious but I somehow felt that the fates were against us. I could neither credit such happiness, nor, as the days passed, feel justified in embracing it at the expense of another's unhappiness.' He will marry the cousin. Then there had still been time for F. to forestall this. And no doubt he, too, had waited – waited in vain for a telegram, for release, for a letter at least in reply to one it was now two years too late to answer.

18

'Games of chess now seem to me utterly unreal.' No clients; no peep out of Egglestone. And none out of me with, on the first day of August, a first taste, tang of autumn in the air. The blue hills have shed their veils, blown away by a breeze that's intoxicatingly fresh. All sharpened, clear, *alive* as I cross the scabious field, in fact now in possession of the harebells, almost invisibly small as these are, bells of blue church glass. . . .

As I'm thinking this it suddenly breaks in – that extraordinary dream I had, was it last night? I was walking through this same field, but yellow and blue and pink with those giant flowers, all like daisies children draw. And where Lobb's House is, should have been, was our house – and Vivers, *Vivers and the Wrecker living in it.*

With the feel of the dream as strong as if I'd only now woken from it (like the dream when I had measles and woke up sobbing, and couldn't explain that Louise had fallen – I'd pushed her – off the moon, and no one could convince me that she hadn't), I flee home in a panic.

The P.E.'s in the bathroom, shaving with a face-towel round his neck. Shaken, supposing that Tom, at the least, has been gored to death by the bull, he puts down his razor as gasping I get it out. But already, as I tell it, it's ceasing to be real; already, still wiping my eyes, I'm starting to laugh, to feel an utter fool. The P.E., though, knows about nightmares; and says: 'You've been overdoing it, sweetheart.'

Then, switching his mouth to one side, about to shave his upper lip, says 'Would it be such a tragedy?'

Would what be? If it happened. If Vivers did buy: 'Would you really mind it so very much?'

Mind the Wrecker, mind Suzette living in our house! Of course I'd mind! Why would I mind so much? Because she's a Wrecker. . . . I'm on the point of shouting. Insouciance, laissez-faire, I'm off to the beck.

No, take the car. That'll show him. He hates being without the car; it makes him feel trapped if he can't get out. And there'll be no snoozing today, my lad, just plenty of time to think. And do some work on your own insouciance.

Slam the door of the car. Fish in my bag for car-keys. They aren't there. They must be. They aren't.

He must have heard the car-door slam. I wish he'd come down and say . . . laughing say, 'Here are your car-keys, sweetheart.'

He doesn't come. That's fixed it. Besides I've found the car-keys. There's no way out. I'll have to go. Where?

Anywhere. First up the drive. Fast, recklessly fast. Then where? It doesn't matter where.

He loves her. He loves me not. He wants her to have the house, wants to give her our house, even married to Vivers.

'You can't leave this house. I so love this house.' He loves her so much he wants her to have *our* house.

'Vivers travels a lot.' And with Vivers away leading his 'interesting life', it would be quite like old times. He could still always drop in, move in come to that. *Ménage à trois. Mariage à la mode.*

I'm up on the open moor now. I've only gone two miles; I could still go back. He doesn't want me back. If he did he wouldn't have let me go.

It's over. There's no going back.

Where can I go? It doesn't matter where.

It will never matter ever again.

Somewhere, anywhere off these hills. Where I can think; I'll have to. And I can't here. It's too near home. Near the bone.

That small dulcet valley. . . . The one with the derelict chapel? Yes; out of the wind. I'll go there.

It's a sweet place. But the wrong one. I can't think here either, can't recapture what I needed to think. Think out.

The need ceases among these tilting gravestones, growing so quietly in the flowering grass. Death growing into life, growing into grass, into the life of grass. No, into life. Waiting to tilt its faded statement over your pain, your love.

Over age, youth, beauty, Braudel.

Don't think. No, it's pointless. Thinking changes nothing: 'The knowledge imposes a pattern and falsifies'.

It was false anyway.

He saw that card. He's known all along about Vivers.

Get up and tour the tombstones, deciphering their inscriptions. Fall to thinking about 'obituaries': that 'a man acquires a "life-story" only after death. Before this he may possibly and only possess an inner pattern, to which he alone has access.'

My husband certainly kept the pattern dark.

> In the middle, not only in the middle of the way
> But all the way, in a dark wood. . . .

Yes, I couldn't see the wood for the trees. But I'm through and out of the wood now. It's light and pale and green like ouzo here, the washed-out green of uncut grass, a washed-out water-colour which, back in my place by the wall, nettles apart, suits me perfectly. The weakest of water-colours, all I can take, just about my form.

I suppose it's this that, perversely it seems, throws up the thought of my 'novel' (a thought which could hardly be more gratuitous), throwing into relief its absurd melodrama. Hopelessly dated. The *Rebecca* vintage.

Well I'm obviously not a Le Carré, but even given my

vintage, what an odd subject. How did I hit upon it? That Mother! No, it's obvious – the duplicity, treachery. Unconsciously I knew and symbolized.

The Wrecker at the foot of my 'pond'. Her destructiveness.

But how did she get, did I let her, into my pond, to tangle with the weeds, surface like Calypso? When I certainly didn't 'forget' her; one couldn't forget.

The Mother's plight – age, love. And I gave her no vestige of pity. Which is why it's ham, over-acted.

I've made her into a threatening shade, a vulture, shadow not substance.

How did I let the Wrecker into my pond?

Possibly she slipped in like a trout, as herself a shadow. Possibly the substance eluded me.

Or possibly my pond was her habitat.

Shake off the ouzo. Think. Have I been destructive? Yes, wasn't that why the Wrecker got in: the brass bed bounding, resounding; the bell tolls for thee; up that drive fast, recklessly fast?

'Melodrama'. The self-indulgence of this – don't you see? Yes, I'm starting to see.

It's too late.

> For the pattern is new in every moment
> And every moment is a new and shocking
> Valuation of all we have been. . . .

Too new and too damning. I'll have to get out of here. Somewhere where I can get a fresh valuation.

In that case you'll have to go back. One can never go back. No, Tuscany, Greece, Spain – on my own.

Taking in London – and Jason:

'The causes of human action are invariably, immeasurably more complex than our subsequent explanations of them.'

155

What if it's true? There'll be no point in Spain. So why not risk going back? What have I got to lose? Listen, the pattern is new in every moment.

'Sweetheart!' His arms go round me. 'Thank God! Where have you been?'

Shake off his arms. 'Somewhere where I could think. I've only come for my passport.'

'It's upstairs. They're both out of date. I've just checked.'

So *he's* thinking of checking out. To Mexico I suppose.

'Listen, sit down. We've got to talk about this.'

'I need something to eat.'

'I'll get you some bread and cheese.'

'I'll get it myself.'

'Sweetheart, we've got to talk.'

'About Vivers, I suppose, wanting to buy this house. You've known all the time about Vivers, haven't you?'

'Yes, for some months.'

'Well, I've known, put up with it for years. Swallowed my pride and put up with you being besotted about Suzette. What I can't swallow is your dishonesty.'

He's angry now. 'Firstly I'm not besotted about Suzette. You don't know the facts; you never have. You can't take them on. I've always protected, had to protect you from them. I made a mistake. What the hell do you think I've been doing in Belldale? Thinking of you; trying to stave her off, trying to spare your feelings, grotesque as these seemed to me. And then, when this failed, what do you think I've done? Lain upstairs still wondering how best to spare you – waiting on you for the right moment. Waiting as always, all our married life, I've had to do. Waiting on your ups and downs, your moods. It's not the right moment now, but you'll have to face it. Vivers has not only put down the full price, but more,

156

enough to cover Egglestone's cut. It's not an offer we can reject. For the first time in our lives we'll be free from worry. Free to go wherever we want.'

There's nowhere I want to go.

'In that case I've waited in vain.'

No, wait for me.

It's going to be a long wait though, one that may never end.

'For the first time in our lives we'll be free from worry. Free [the irony of it!] to go wherever we want.' How can I possibly want to go anywhere, crippled by the sense that I've forfeited his respect? 'Always, all our married life' he said. Deadly words. The whole of our past cancelled at a stroke, like a tree struck dead by lightning – Ischia, Ely, love in a tent camping with the children in the rain, love in bedsocks in the Apennines. . . .

I thought we were happy, idyllically happy.

We were idyllically happy.

Still happy here in bedsocks in the Pennines.

The shock will fade, but the rift perhaps never completely heal. 'And we shall be changed'. No, I can't bear it!

I swear we were happy. In that case can't we be happy again? It's up to me. I'll never be happy again.

I've been too near the edge, perilously near, near enough to learn about precipices, fells, cliffs of fall. . . .

And now I'm still on the edge. Of the Room in the Field? '"So you see it won't be so bad"'. What won't be? Moving. Moving into what I do not know.

I've already moved into this. No, you're in the photographer's dark-room, where gradually you will see the plate emerge, not in his words, beneath these, like trees reflected in water.

This is your mute motionless winter's day.

You couldn't enter the dark-room of your own volition. It was death, don't you see, that barred your way, the way that leads to Lermontov. You couldn't see ahead. You yourself erected that paling-fence.

What if I did? The subject doesn't faintly interest me. What does? What will emerge from under his words. 'In that case I've waited in vain!' Don't you see it's a cry of despair? Won't you, can't you see that he loves you still?

He's thinking of France, a place near the sea, where the winters are warm enough, Jason says, to bathe on Christmas Day.

Not thinking about the Wrecker. Thinking about *us*. So there's no point in my thinking about her either.

There was never any point. . . . Yes, there was a point. As I thought in that graveyard. And as he's confirmed.

Today I halt, hover a trifle unsteadily by the beck, somehow haul myself through the stile in the wall and on between my blue hills, blue perimeters (no fictive 'Andes captive in their train').

Still as Darby and Joan on the edge? Of age, cancer, grief? Yes, but it seems we've always been on the edge. Perhaps it's the only valid place, the only place one can be.

Into the blue – the only place to go.